If I Had Wheels or Love

COLLECTED POEMS

of

VASSAR MILLER

If I Had

Southern Methodist University Press / *Dallas*

Wheels or Love

COLLECTED
POEMS
OF
VASSAR
MILLER/

With an Introduction by

GEORGE GARRETT

Copyright © 1991 by Vassar Miller
Introduction copyright © 1991 by George Garrett
All rights reserved
Printed in the United States of America

First edition, 1991

*Grateful acknowledgment is made for permission to re-
print the following published works by Vassar Miller:*

The texts of *Adam's Footprint* (copyright © 1956 by Vas-
sar Miller) and *Struggling to Swim on Concrete* (copyright
© 1984 by Vassar Miller) are reprinted with the permis-
sion of New Orleans Poetry Journal Press.
Wage War on Silence was first published by Wesleyan
University Press in 1960, *My Bones Being Wiser* in 1963,
Onions and Roses in 1968. They are reprinted by
permission.
The text of *If I Could Sleep Deeply Enough*, Poems, by
Vassar Miller, is reprinted with the permission of Liveright
Publishing Corporation. Copyright © 1968, 1972, 1973,
1974 by Vassar Miller.
The texts of *Small Change* (copyright © 1976 by Vassar
Miller) and *Approaching Nada* (copyright © 1977 by
Vassar Miller) are reprinted with the permission of Wings
Press.
The text of "The Sun Has No History" from *Selected and
New Poems, 1950–1980* is reprinted with the permission
of Latitudes Press. Copyright © 1981 by Vassar Miller.

Library of Congress Cataloging-in-Publication Data
Miller, Vassar.
    If I had wheels or love: collected poems of Vassar
Miller/with an introduction by George Garrett.—
1st ed.
        p.   cm.
    Includes indexes.
    ISBN 0-87074-315-5 (cloth).—ISBN 0-87074-316-3
(paper)
    I. Title.
PS3525.I5635I45   1991   90-52660
811'.54—dc20

Photo by Maud Lipscomb
Design by Whitehead & Whitehead

For
　Mary Jean Irion
　　and
　　　Maxine Cassin

Contents

MY BONES BEING WISER

xi

Introduction

*F*OR MORE than thirty years, more than half my life so far, and for all my time as a writer, I have been well aware of and an admirer of Vassar Miller's poetry. Her first book, *Adam's Footprint* (1956), came along a year before my own first collection. Her name and her work were to be found in the enviable best of the magazines of that time—in *Accent, The Beloit Poetry Journal, The Hopkins Review, The New Orleans Poetry Journal, Prairie Schooner,* and others. That was a little surprising, for, as ever and always, each of those magazines had its own distinct way and its own crew of regular contributors. Clearly, from the beginning, Vassar Miller belonged to no school or crew, representing no faction or fashion—except, perhaps, the fashion of admirable excellence that made her work appropriately at home in any of these places. Her poems were gracefully formal, moving at ease among a variety of stanzas and forms, both traditional and original. The voice, from the outset, was all her own, clear, accessible, often close to the edges of pure song, willing and able to assume an eloquence that was rare (then or now) without at the same time losing touch with the power and glory of common American speech. And the substance of all this, the core and the center, was religious—Christian, as knotty and complex in thought and image as any of the seventeenth-century Metaphysicals, whom we were all reading and studying at that time; yet, at the same time, as luminous and playfully profound as the finest moments of George Herbert, whose work we did not study as much as we ought to have. From the poems you would have known that her belief, though sorely tested and touched with pain (as Jacob was wounded by his angel at the river's edge), was firm and auspicious and utterly unsentimental. The nearest thing to the voice and vision of Vassar Miller, an analogous quality with some subtle differences, could be found in the early stories of Flannery O'Connor, which were just then beginning to bear witness in the literary magazines. Thomas Merton was much in mind in those days, too; and he is a presence, sometimes named, in the poetry of Vassar Miller.

The genuinely religious experience, dealt with directly by a living artist of the first rank, was as astonishing then as it is now or any time; shocking, really, in our secular and self-absorbed times. I have in hand a recent letter from the poet and novelist R. H. W. Dillard, whose separate experience with the poems of Vassar Miller, beginning a little later with her third book, is close enough to my own to be spooky.

> It has been twenty-six years since I first found and read Vassar Miller's *My Bones Being Wiser*, and I can still remember the almost visceral shock I felt reading a genuinely religious poetry that was neither pietistic nor cooly, fashionably and distantly intellectual, but was rather a fully felt, fully expressed and fully crafted poetry of intense belief. And I still turn to Vassar Miller's poetry when I become discouraged from reading too many contemporary poems that are merely exercises in anecdotal self regard or are flights of linguistic fancy completely detached from hard fact or harder belief. It always works, and I recover my faith in a poetry that actually *matters.*

Another younger poet, Kelly Cherry, has also written to me recently about the impact of Vassar Miller's poetry upon herself. Something of the fire and excitement of the poetry, as it works upon the consciousness and being of an alert reader, is aptly evoked by Kelly Cherry:

> In her best poems, Vassar Miller launches language like a satellite, sending a probe into the inner space of moral consciousness and religious awe. Only a writer unafraid to explore the most difficult paradoxes of existence could apostrophize God as ". . . Word, in whom our wordiness dissolves, / When we have not a prayer except ourselves."

Only a writer unafraid to admit human need and limitation could write, so startlingly frankly, "I wish I could call my mother / or eat death like candy." Let us say it again. This is poetry "wholly / out of faith furnaced, fired by doubt"; in short, a poetry wrestling with itself like an angel.

Never part of any literary fashion show, Vassar Miller's poetry was perhaps more modestly at home in the literary neighborhood of the late 1950s when others, often with much less success, were working within the fences of formal verse. After that, come the 1960s and much else, and American poetry went off in all directions at once, as if in prophetic fulfillment of Vassar Miller's picture of the world Columbus left behind, in "Columbus Dying": "men creeping to and fro, / Gum-footed flies glued to a spinning ball." Vassar Miller's work changed, too, but not by discarding her aesthetic ways and means or denying where she had been. She expanded her craft to include freer and easier verses when they were needed, yet all the while continuing to explore the possibilities of singing and dancing in strict forms. And, in subject, bit by bit over the years, shyly reducing the distance between the poet and herself until she came to be able to come face to face with the wounded and handicapped self of childhood, with the fallibility and weakness of others, kith and kin, friends and strangers, who may have meant well enough but who often worked harm. There is nothing "confessional" here, but there is nothing hidden or denied either. On the one hand she expanded her art to include the personal and even the ordinary. On the other she has continued, as she began, mining deeper and deeper the dark places of the spirit, always admitting that the poet, herself, is not, finally, the same being as the mystic since (as she writes in "Approaching Nada") "the poet like the mouse will scuttle / clean to the border / of the ineffable, / then scurry back / with tidbits of the Vision." The tidbits she brings us back shine like precious stones in a bright light.

Through all the years Vassar Miller has been faithful to her vision, growing and changing as a poet yet, remarkably, not losing touch with the first self, the original poet of *Adam's Footprint*, although that younger self (like mine and yours) has vanished, as she says in the recent poem "Spring Singsong": "my younger self's lost, lost / and hunches down in between yesterday's buildings / all hunkering down / among slenderest flowers of steel."

This book will give us the whole scope of Vassar Miller's art from then to now. And even though her place among our best has been long since earned, one is entitled to hope that the book will bring her new recognition and new readers. There is so much to discover here. Henry Taylor, himself a recent Pulitzer Prize–winner, has written to me about his discovery of the poems of Vassar Miller:

> When I was in college, I was always discovering new poets, and some of them became a permanent part of my life. Some of them, I guess, I re-read now and make excuses for my youthful enthusiasm. And a few others make for occasionally interesting nostalgia trips. And a few, like Vassar Miller, seem to have gotten better as the years added up. What I liked then was the honesty and her gift with forms. I still like that and am closer now to an understanding of her faithfulness and her faith.

 I have no doubt at all that somewhere there is a very young person, maybe even an unformed poet, who will sooner or later pick up this new book and read in it and be moved and changed for good. It has already happened to several generations of us and I am confident that the spell, the magic of it, will work in the future, in a world we can only vaguely imagine. The publication of this book is a cause for joyous celebration, then. On behalf of many others I salute Vassar Miller and wish her well in all things, believing without doubt or question the triumphant assertion found in her lovely new villanelle "If I Had Wheels Or Love":

> *Deep in the shadows where I found the way*
> *I could make prayers or poems on and on.*

George Garrett

Adam's
Footprint
1956

Adam's Footprint

Once as a child I loved to hop
On round plump bugs and make them stop
Before they crossed a certain crack.
My bantam brawn could turn them back,
My crooked step wrenched straight to kill
Live pods that then screwed tight and still.

Small sinner, stripping boughs of pears,
Shinnied past sweet and wholesome airs,
How could a tree be so unclean?
Nobody knows but Augustine.
He nuzzled pears from dam-sin's dugs—
And I scrunched roly-poly bugs.

No wolf's imprint or tiger's trace
Does Christ hunt down to catch with grace
In nets of love the devious preys
Whose feet go softly all their days:
The foot of Adam leaves the mark
Of some child scrabbling in the dark.

Alternatives

What will assuage this dog-self of his hunger,
Pawing among the garbage heaps, his pang
Gouging through caverns of his guts like anger
Denied the dignity of cause and tongue?
Quivering beneath his gluttonies bedrocked
In belly and in blood, the jig and jerk
Of titillated nerves tend to obstruct
A transcendental nuance in his bark.
So, when he prays, his whining never bounces
Beyond the roof of ego; should he fit
His grunts to rhyme, a new Narcissus minces
Before the mirror, ogling his own snout.
Deprived of rutting, poetry, and prayer—
He takes a nap or plays some solitaire.

Apology

My mortal love's a rabbit skin
That will not reach around your bones
To charm the chill, to wrap you in
Against the wind whose undertones
Are death, or snow whose flakes are stones.
My word will never do for thread
To knit you garments snug and tight
Though I would fold you foot and head
Against the frost-fangs of the night
Killing whatever rose they bite.
My will is not enough to stretch
The tattered pelt around us two.
Pity, with each of us a wretch,
Comes dyed my hurt's deceitful hue
As rag for me, not robe for you.
The only cover from heart's weather,
The only comfort under which
Our naked souls may crouch together
Only immortal love, all-rich
In warmer wool than fleece, can stitch.

Autumnal Spring Song

When autumn wounds the bough
And bleeds me white and shaken,
Forbear to tell me how
The spring must reawaken
    And the trees bloom on forever,
    But with the same leaves never.

When autumn smears the sheen
Of leaf-lace, nature's lore
Affirms each season's green
To shimmer as before
    While the trees bloom on forever.
    But with the same leaves? Never.

When every branch is whole
The bitter sword of spring
Will scar the forest's soul
And mine remembering
    That the trees bloom on forever,
    But with the same leaves never.

Lord, You must comfort me
When woods are autumn's spoil,
Yet with another Tree
Unnourished by the soil
    Whence the trees bloom on forever,
    But with the same leaves never.

Ballade of Blind Alleys

The universal itch, no less
Whether in body, heart, or mind,
Grows putrid with the same excess
Of lust unslaked and unresigned.
For those who wait and those who wind
The coil of labor, those who drive
Engines or dreams have yet to find
How to escape from life alive.

The arid cot, the humid press
Of hairs and arms and legs entwined
Both fence away the wilderness
Of multitudes that grunt and grind;
In both the pariah soul has pined
To skin and bones which half survive,
Learning no better than his kind
How to escape from life alive.

The ice-eyed savants only guess.
Soaring, they leave the truth behind;
Parading, they cannot progress,
Sliding and slipping on the rind
Of contradiction, disinclined
To indicate, should they arrive
Even at alleys dark and blind,
How to escape from life alive.

ENVOY

Lord, whom denying we confess,
Teach us—lest pitfalls we contrive
But catch us for the pantheress—
How to escape from life alive!

Beside a Deathbed

Her spirit hiding among skin and bones
In willingness and wariness waits death
Like hares that peer from corners of their pens
Lured by a curiosity, yet loath.
Her eyes meet bed, chair, face, but do not focus,
As if these objects, heretofore mere shade,
Have caught up with their shadows. Things that wake us
Upon her eyelids heap a heavy load.
As straws pierce rock, our words reach where she lies,
Heedless of our cheerfulness or condolence.
Uncaring how our chatter ebbs or flows,
She catches the first syllable of silence.
So true the craftsman, memory, in lying
She will be less a stranger dead than dying.

Bout with Burning

I have tossed hours upon the tides of fever,
Upon the billows of my blood have ridden,
Where fish of fancy teem as neither river
Nor ocean spawns from India to Sweden.
Here while my boat of body burnt has drifted
Along her sides crawled tentacles of crabs
Sliming her timbers; on the waves upwafted
Crept water rats to gnaw her ropes and ribs.
Crashing, she has dived, her portholes choking
With weed and ooze, the swirls of black and green
Gulping her inch by inch, the seagulls' shrieking
Sieved depth through depth to silence. Till blast-blown,
I in my wreck beyond storm's charge and churning
Have waked marooned upon the coasts of morning.

The Cat

Gliding through the hallways like a huge gray moth,
Moving like a daemon from an ancient myth,
Never quite a god and never quite a devil,
The cat feigns to cater to our human drivel:

Here nice kitty-kitty, spinster's pride and pet.
(Wasn't that he sunning by her flower pot?)
Now he laps his cream or rubs the hand that feeds him,
Now he's disappeared where his own shadow hides him.

If he comes no more, O burrow in your pillow,
Trembling, meager mortal, for your weird bedfellow.
Do not think him strayed when by his mystic license
He has merely dwindled to his eerie essence.

He is not encoffined in his claws and fur.
Where he is or is not, tell us you who fear
Never cat alive, so you boast with mocking mouth,
As gliding through the halls weaves a huge gray moth.

Ceremony

I can preserve your letters, not your love
As I might keep your likeness, not your life
For souvenir. Shades fluttered on and off
The wall proclaim at least that they derive
From substances, while these at most,
These scrawls, are only charms invoked upon
My grief and loneliness, but grace alone
Is the one means of grace—and grace is lost.
So, offering these follies up, these tokens
Of tokens in this fable of a fire
Upon an altar no man's structure likens,
I gesture beyond gesture to explore
For sign or symbol till the lack of any
Has clothed my nakedness in ceremony.

Christmas Mourning

On Christmas Day I weep
Good Friday to rejoice.
I watch the Child asleep.
Does He half dream the choice
The Man must make and keep?

At Christmastime I sigh
For my Good Friday hope.
Outflung the Child's arms lie
To span in their brief scope
The death the Man must die.

Come Christmastide I groan
To hear Good Friday's pealing.
The Man, racked to the bone,
Has made His hurt my healing,
Has made my ache His own.

Slay me, pierced to the core
With Christmas penitence
So I who, new-born, soar
To that Child's innocence,
May wound the Man no more.

Columbus Dying

His men in fever, scabs, and hunger pains—
He found a world and put to scorn his scorners.
Yet having learned the living sea contains
No dragons gnawing on drowned sailors' brains,
He missed the angels guarding the four corners,
And begged that he be buried with his chains

In token that he'd sworn to serve as thrall
His vision of men creeping to and fro,
Gum-footed flies glued to a spinning ball.
Whether they tumble off earth's edge or crawl
Till dropped dead in their tracks from vertigo,
He deemed would make no difference at all.

Consolations of Relativity

Quicksilver nerves awry, you inch
Your wheelchair on from here to yonder
With muscles like a fist whose clinch
Keeps itself captive. Yet why squander
Your admiration to aver
My feet are heeled with lightning's wings,
My hands merged into moth-gray blurs
Of harpist fingers over strings!

The stars competing in their race,
With one another for sole measure,
Flash neither gaucherie nor grace,
Neither celerity nor leisure.
Galactic seas stagnate unrippled,
For—being deadlocked in the groove
Of their own motion—more than crippled,
Even the fleetest never move.

Contingencies

My breath-brief friend, when more days tumble
Between us now than linked me to you,
Why does the dart of your death tremble
Through me who may no longer know you?

More than my own your life was hapless;
Deeper the spear in your heart thrust.
You might have been, our fates yet shapeless,
A child I nourished from my breast.

Such fascination of the fleeting
Was yours, you might have been while still
Our forms escaped the future's witting
The prince of my impossible.

But since all molten morrows harden
To history, their hazards stolen,
You were the music with this burden:
A snowflake in the desert fallen.

Crone's Cradle-Song

Hushed hands, before you fumble
Into knot and gnarl,
Fixed feet, before you stumble
Weaving steps asnarl—
    Much prefer
    Stillness without stir.

Mute mouth, before you break
Song against your tongue,
Lax lips, before you make
Music wried-and-wrung—
    Silence dance
    Down such dissonance!

Body, before you race
Brain and blood and breath
Against the grain of grace,
Bend birth back to death—
    Lullaby,
    Given leave to die.

Epitaph for a Cripple

Feet that, floundering, go
No way of your own will—
Numb with eternity
You now have gained your goal.

Fingers writhed from weaving
Like crabs with claws torn loose—
You mold in your unmoving
The perfect shape of peace.

Tongue entangled in
The ravels of confusion—
You have learned silence soon,
The language of precision.

Body, wry reproach
To athlete mind, lie down—
Your lubber's limbs here couch
Graced with the state of stone.

Epithalamium

Crept side by side beyond the thresh
And throb of noise, do not come near it,
But bind the bandage of the flesh
Upon the open wound of spirit.

Crouched in the corner of your lust,
Doctor your hurts till by the prod
Of some next moment you are thrust
Against the cauteries of God.

Before He burns and scars to kill
Infection, God, who is the cleaver
Of bone from bone to cure the ill,
Bids you alleviate the fever.

Faintly and from Far Away

Between the wheeze of her torpor and the wind of her falling,
Between the whey of her face and the snow of its blanching,
Between the vacuum of her monotone and the void of its stilling
Was only the difference between the cicadas on a summer
    afternoon
And their declining into the bottom of evening,
Only the difference between the sparrows pecking the rock of
    silence
And the rock of silence itself.

Father, rememberer of sparrows and dullards,
Each of us cries, even as she, from some twig of a cross:
    Remember me Lord. Before it swoops me up, feather
    The hawk of the world's forgetting with the down of Your
    memory.

Fantasy on the Resurrection

Flaws cling to flesh as dews cling to a rose:
The cripples limp as though they would prolong,
Walking, a waltz; the deaf ears, opened, close
As if their convolutions hoard all song;
The blind eyes keep half shut as if to fold
A vision fast men never glimpse by staring;
Against their will the mute lips move that hold
A language which was never tongue's for sharing.
Shocked shag of earth and everything thereunder
Turned inside out—the nail-gnarled have caught Heaven
Like a bright ball. Not in their reknit wonder,
But in their wounds lies Christ's sprung grace engraven—
Not in the body lighter than word spoken,
But in the side still breached, the hands still broken.

The Final Hunger

Hurl down the nerve-gnarled body hurtling head-
Long into sworls of shade-hush. Plummeting, keep
The latch of eyelids shut and so outleap
Care's claws. Arms, legs, abandon grace and spread
Your spent sprawl—glutton ravening to be fed
With fats, creams, fruits, meats, spice that heavyheap
The hands, that golden-gloss the flesh, of sleep,
Sleep, the sole lover that I take to bed.

But they couch crouching in the darkness, city
Of wakefulness uncaptured by assaulting—
Senses by sleep unravished and unwon.
Sun-sword night-sheathed, lie never between (have pity!)
Between me and my love, between me and the vaulting
Down the dense sweetness of oblivion.

Incognito

FOR TRIXIE MOORE

Why did you come, you with your great wings drooped,
Who could not fly and found no way to crawl?
But being caught and cramped and clogged and cropped,
You lagged behind us in our cacklers' school;
Fitted your breadth along our narrow need
And, ill-assorting with it, never saw
How you were measured to a line unflawed,
Marked out by new dimensions.
                              Now we see.
Our garbled grammar held your song ensnared.
Ours was a barbarous croak with which you struggled,
The delicate trills deep in your throat so slurred.
We know you now, you with your bright wings draggled—
Valiant to live in love, image most regal
With red heart hue of Him, Christ, cross-caged eagle.

Invocation to Bacchus Grown Old

Come weave me out of wine
A fabric frail and fine;
Come wrap me well within
Its bubble's rosy skin
So delicate a breath
May tear its tender sheath,
With me so poised past stir
No darker sepulchre
Could bury me deep under
The earth from snarl of thunder.
Since on its fragile woof
The ancient stamp of hoof,
Though light as dewdrop's clatter
Would, beating, bruise and shatter;
Since you and I and time
Have worn away our prime
Beyond all tug of lust
In either groin or ghost
Wherefore the grape is broken
In low or lofty token;
Since we're too old to leap—
No prayer of mine shall keep
Your ear except for sleep.

Love Song out of Nothing

You, being less than either dew or frost
Which sun can melt, are deader than the dead
Who once at least had life. You never fled
Because you never came, were never lost
From me since never held; you cannot boast
Of having been a whole, so leave no shred,
No footprint on the ground you did not tread.
For where no flesh has been there is no ghost.

Mirage upon the desert of my mind
Are you to me who walked alone before
You formed from crooked heat waves of my thought.
For when I mourn the want of you, I find
I only mourn a part of me, no more,
Who, minus you, am nothing but a nought.

Made Flesh

Cleanse me in mathematics, not in blood.
Lay its chill chasteness tangent to my flesh.
A square is no Pandora's Box of dread;
A circle is not circumscribed to crush.
Constructing angles of a polygon
Wider than worlds rouses no nation's rancor—
Spaceless geometry deprives no man
Upon the postulate, "In this sign conquer."
Yet, disciplined by eye, ruled off by pen,
Or dropped from brain to hand, no line flows straight.
A circle may assume the loop of chain,
A square incarnate in the jaw hate-set.
Therefore, made wood, two lines by intersection
Form the contortion of the Crucifixion.

The Magnitude of Zero

Trudge up and down time's stone metropolis
Though years or only hours have run their race
Since I last breathed, its concrete holds no trace
Where my foot fell. In some eye catch, yet miss
The light is hinted, my small emphasis.
Then you who watch a differing measure chase
My shadow-music from the stranger's face
Murmur Vedantist-style, "Neti. Not this."

No one's first citizen so briefly played
On flesh and bone. I quail at my own cost.
Hand-wrought, once broken, never knitted back—
Here, Love, am I (like diamond or jade,
Neither one more than trash except when lost)
Whom death splays huge upon my nothing's rack.

Mirror for a Lady

TO B. M. E.

Her grace informs her like her soul,
Though in what manner who can tell?
Neither as fruit lies in a bowl,
Nor yet as water fills a well—
But more as calm imbues her smile,
More as a cello lifts and falls
Within her voice when for a while
We, too, belong within her halls
Wherein the fustian of our ways
Shimmers to satins of her poise,
Wherein the measures of her phrase
In their own notes absorb our noise.
For she, by merit of whose glance
Our discords merge in polyphony,
Has wrought an ease of elegance
And made a home of ceremony.

The New Icarus

Slip off the husk of gravity to lie
Bedded with wind; float on a whimsy, lift
Upon a wish: your bow's own arrow, rift
Newton's decorum—only then you fly.
But naked. No false-feathered fool, you try
Dalliance with heights, nor, plumed with metal, shift
And shear the clouds, imperiling lark and swift
And all bridal-bowered in the sky.

Your wreck of bone, barred their delight's dominions,
Lacking their formula for flight, holds imaged
Those alps of air no eagle's wing can quell.
With arms flung crosswise, pinioned to wooden pinions,
You, in one motion plucked and crimson-plumaged,
Outsoar all Heaven, plummeting all Hell.

No Return

Once over summer streams the ice-crusts harden,
No one can wade therein to wash his feet
Thence to go flying after nymphs that fleet
Naked and nimble through the woods. Time's warden
Has locked them all (or is it us?) past pardon.
Yet freed, we could not find the path that beat
Toward—call it any name—fauns, home, retreat;
For there is no returning to that garden.

No, not to Adam's. We must keep our own,
Remembering. In Eden's greenery
God walked. While in our garden rocks are brown
With His dried blood where He has crouched to groan.
Our apples rotted, only His crosstree
Bears crimson fruit. But no hand plucks it down.

Nuptial Benediction

Though beauty has not made your bed
And grace has not composed your limbs,
Your lust with eyes put out has led
Your steps; though few of Cupid's whims
You can obey like love's athletes,
Though you disrobe, so some might guess,
For crosses, not for marriage sheets,
Close here the gash of loneliness
Like nimbler lovers; though you urge
Your passion on with less precision—
May your twin blindnesses now merge
In one beatitude of vision.

Paradox

Mild yoke of Christ, most harsh to me not bearing,
You bruise the neck that balks, the hands that break you;
Sweet bread and wine, bitter to me not sharing,
You scar and scorch the throat that will not take you;
Mount where He taught, you cripple feet not bloody
From your sharp flints of eight-fold benediction;
Bright cross, most shameful stripped of the stripped body,
You crucify me safe from crucifixion:
Yet I, who am my own dilemma, jolting
My mind with thought lest it unthink its stiffness,
Rise to revolt against my own revolting.
Blind me to blindness, deafen me to deafness.
So will Your gifts of sight and hearing plunder
My eyes with lightning and my ears with thunder.

Prayer against Two Perils

How may your poor child, father, dare surmise
The shape of grief your death would wear, or know
How tears, once wasted over trifles, flow
(If storms of agony do not capsize
Custom's old crates), or how these very eyes
Should gaze along a road you did not go?
But since all means are impotent to show,
All means save one, may you not make me wise.

Yet if, most erudite in pain and loss
From measuring barefoot, jag by jag, their earth,
You swear the lack of me deserves your bother
Or dream such dismal desert fit to cross,
Your blood splashed over clods of fancied worth,
May I not make you wise, poor child, my father.

A Prayer for Prayer

This bone of honesty wedged in my throat
Bars my prayer passage so that I can neither
Cough up the bone nor swallow down the words.
How shall I take my heart into my mouth
When the two cramp each other? Deepen and soften
Alike my clanging clapper of a tongue
To the precise proportion of my meaning?
For if I took the truth upon my lips,
Its nitric would devour them. If I learned
The way to form the labials of silence,
My teeth of thought would gnaw them into pulp.
Christ, from the pincers, speech and dumbness, never
Absolve me till I am dissolved, but dangle
Me and my word over the flame and fuse us,
A lesser word-made-flesh, enunciated
Clean to the bitter syllable of blood.

Puritan Delight

The feet that can define
Their proper elegance
Practice the sparseness of a line
Till they forget to dance.

The tones that scale the reach
Of melody belong
Under the discipline of speech
And have no need of song.

The fingers kept by grace
Display with each devotion
To driving nails or netting lace
The diamonds of motion.

Then clear away incense
From movement, sound, and sight;
Let their austerity teach whence
Comes Puritan delight.

Reciprocity

You who would sorrow even for a token
Of hurt in me no less than you would grieve
For seeing me with my whole body broken
And long no less to solace and relieve;
You who, as though you wished me mere Good Morning,
Would smash your heart upon the hardest stones
Of my distress as when you once, unscorning,
Would sleep upon the margin of my moans—
I yield my want, this house of gutted portals,
All to your want, I yield this ravaged stack,
In testimony that between two mortals
No gift may be except a giving back.
What present could I make you from what skill
When your one need is me to need you still?

Rescue

Washed on the sands of waking,
Up from the tides of sleep—
The body slackened and aching,
Swaying from tug and sweep
Of the kelp that, glued around it
Like tentacles, have bound it
And dragged it deep to deep.

Down where the self is sheathed in
Satins of nakedness,
Where the body lies enwreathed in
Only its own caress,
Drifting through liquid meadows.
Quick! Cover it with shadows.
Veil it in decent dress.

The beach's grit and pebbles
Will prick the nerves aware,
Untune the ear to the trebles
Shrilling their airless air.
With gull's rasp of rousing
Jar the limbs loose from drowsing
Soon, or they may not care.

Revival

FOR N. C.

Good Brother Botts through gesture and gyration
Of fervor flung himself, and when he'd finished,
We bellowed out a hymn of invitation
In hopes that Hell's domain might be diminished.

When we had sung the final verse, he boomed,
"Before the congregation starts disbandin',
That we may win tonight some soul who's doomed—
You saved sit down, you unsaved remain standin'."

Proclaiming then with one collective bump
(Each lamb among us haughtier than a Roman)
How grace had cushioned every pious rump,
We plopped, all but a solitary woman,

Defying, like a child man's broils have chosen,
Our vice and virtue stewed to one stale shred;
Her face, a hurricane of meekness frozen
Stubborn as stone she'd scorn to give for bread.

Botts wheedled her with Heaven's gaudy gold,
But she'd watched folks limp deathward doubt by doubt.
And when he howled of Hell, she felt as cold
As kitchen stoves are when their fires go out.

Yet while we gawked and Brother Botts decried her,
When One named Truth men tried in Pilate's hall
Rose up, a rapier of flame, beside her,
Nobody saw—and she saw least of all.

Spastic Child

A silk of flame composed his hair to fleck
His cheeks with freckles dappled on his pallor,
Misplaced like cartoons on a pall, to spatter
His chin laced with a silver thread of spittle
His wax doll hands cannot wipe off. Contracting
The muted tragedies of moth and mote
Like crucifixes wrought in ivory,
His tongue, slight mollusk broken in its shell,
Is locked so minnows of his wit may never
Leap playing in our waterspouts of words
For the sheer luxury of diving back
Into the pools of quietude, inlaid
With leaves the autumn-umber of his eyes—
His mind, bright bird, forever trapped in silence.

Taurobolium Twentieth Century

Skyscrapers turn to pillars in a temple;
High heels and oxfords drumming an enslavement
To siren cymbals, devotees here trample
Around me on the altar of the pavement.
Their stare, a mouth stung open with its thirst
To rinse out blindness in my blood, now waits
Until the grape of my bull's heart shall burst,
Transforming them to death's initiates.
I do not grudge them, hoarding like a miser
The secret of how flesh with anguish warps.
For I, too, have gone down to taste the geyser
Of magic bubbling from grotesque and corpse
To come forth unillumined and unstrung
With ignorance still acrid on my tongue.

Unrhetorical Questions

How long till grief profaned by newsboy's braying
Turns sacrament by word ministered and sped?
How long till Shakespeare by poetry made them bread
And wine were Hamlet's flesh and blood decaying?
Do time-drowned tragedies—children who while playing
Fall into wells, or the dead that mourn the dead—
Become sounds sounding nowhere, hearers fled,
Or sea-woods drifting below the sough of swaying?

Is this burlap of pain man cannot toss
Aside but the steel-stitch raveling from the gear
Once bound, wound on His body wrenched awry
The shape of question mark to bear the Cross?
Then did the Cross bear Him that man might hear
All questions asked and answered in God's "Why?"

Unspoken Dialogue

Mine was a question I could never ask;
Yours was the answer you could never tell.
Our conversation hid behind the mask
Of reticence. Death having cleaved our shell
Of silence, silence was our core as well.

You had a secret, one you longed to share
In vain because my muteness was the sieve
Through which it slipped. Yet you who could not spare
Breath to explain, but only breath to live,
You were the secret you could never give.

Neither my question nor your answer matters;
The promise is unkept, the miracle
Unwrought, the song uncaroled, since it shatters
Sooner than shaped. For in heart's tongue-tied lull
The word unspoken proves unspeakable.

Until

Down the cool flue of darkness body flows
From light to light through blindness on and on,
Its weight dissolved to ripplings the wind blows
Through reeds until they lap the beach of dawn.
Down the smooth shaft of night bound over bound
Body plunges past sense towards Morningsfield;
Sprung from the chute of sleep, no car can turn around
Or stop till Tunnelsend is sealed, is sealed
When startled spirit pinned beneath the rubble—
Ears crammed with silence, numbness chaining hands,
Blackness gouging out both eyes—bends double:
Wedged under beams breath bulges, strains, expands
Its bulk until its cramped and strangled vapor
Bursts the pipe of glass, tears the tube of paper.

Waste of Breath

In man—like tea leaves, charms, or crystals—
Speech is but the child who lingers
Waging war with paper pistols,
Catching water in the fingers.

In hide-and-seek with truth, the poet
Lao-tze spied its subtle attar:
"He who chatters does not know it,
He who knows it does not chatter."

Language, he learned, numbs hands forever
Grabbling for God; so I discover
Gloved in words, my thoughts can never
Reach my friend or touch my lover.

For One Long Dead

Death broke the habit such as binds
A life to one unlovely spot;
So, from the corner of our minds
We glimpsed your going—then forgot.

Yet we, not you, have gone the ways
Of ghosts, not one of whom endures
For you, since God's consuming gaze
Has burned our memory from yours.

The Grace of Remembrance

FOR TRIXIE MOORE

May not the little time I had with you
Be swallowed in the whirlpools of the years,
Nor these tears washed away by bitter tears
As dew is lost in rainstorms, though the dew
Has drenched the grasses. May these days, though few,
Not blunt their sharpness like a pair of shears
Dulled upon harder sorrows, shames, and fears,
Or mere monotony, but bite me through.

The sore that opened when I saw you wear
Misfortune like a flower—may it smart
Anew each changeful weather of my soul
To hurt me in my querulous ease and tear
The scabs from memory, from mind and heart,
Because I need such wounds to keep me whole.

Wage
War
On
Silence
1960

Without Ceremony

Except ourselves, we have no other prayer;
Our needs are sores upon our nakedness.
We do not have to name them; we are here.
And You who can make eyes can see no less.
We fall, not on our knees, but on our hearts,
A posture humbler far and more downcast;
While Father Pain instructs us in the arts
Of praying, hunger is the worthiest fast.
We find ourselves where tongues cannot wage war
On silence (farther, mystics never flew)
But on the common wings of what we are,
Borne on the wings of what we bear, toward You,
Oh Word, in whom our wordiness dissolves,
When we have not a prayer except ourselves.

Inviolate

Too long lies the will virgin where she sleeps
Under the room of mind adept at dancing
His gambados upon his floor, entrancing
Attention from the cubicle which keeps
Her flower on ice; however goat-heart leaps
To his own syncopations, so commencing
Flirtations with High Heaven, his lewd prancing
Does not disturb the slumberer in the deeps.

Yet her dead brain is its own troubled dream,
The chill of her body being a frost in blaze,
Her strict gown but a frozen gust. Wherefore,
Swift fingers, rend it, seam from crystal seam;
Bruise, burn, and bare the plump peace of her glaze
Till she lies cradled, cooled, and clothed in fire.

Receiving Communion

The world of stars and space being His bauble,
   He gives me, not a toy
   which were I to destroy
would be no waste that caused Him any trouble,
rather, into my fingers cramped and crooked
   entrusts His body real
   as spitted on a nail
as are my own hands piteous, naked—
because He has no creaking heart's mill grind
   His wheat, nor heart's belief
   play oven; for His loaf
cannot be beaten out or baked by hand—
when He, against the mind's backlash,
   would as a splinter list
   here on my turbulent dust
preventing so all fantasy of flesh.

Cacophony

Her bed as narrow as a cross, she lies
Each night and offers Christ her twisted cries;
But He who has not blessed the soul to plague
The body, has not fitted a round peg
Into a square hole; so, He tells her what
Of old He said to Mary, "Touch Me not,

"If you would keep that which you would enjoy,
For flesh embracing spirit must destroy
Itself, too impotent for what demands
A more tenacious grip than clutching hands.
And, stripping, you remove the wrong robes till
You have undone the buttons of self-will."

So, while the incense of her sighs shall mingle
With sweat, her yearning eye is pure and single
For homely lust as little as for God,
Since, if one night the boilings of her blood
Drowned her devotions, dawn would find her fled,
Cramped by a love no wider than her bed.

Ballad of the Unmiraculous Miracle

Sit under a pine on Christmas Eve,
Heart bruised like a fallen nestling,
And the angels will sing you—no song save
The wind in the branches wrestling.

Peer down a mystical well and see
Far down in its waters mirrored—
The only sign there imaged for me,
My own face mournful and harrowed.

Seek out a stable known of old
And see the oxen kneel—
With me crouched here before the cold
And hunger sharp as steel.

Go wander through the winter snows
And spy the Christmas bud
Unfold itself—the only rose
The brambles bear, my blood.

Like wingless birds are wind and wood,
Well, oxen, flowering bush
Till Christmas Day when I see God
Plumaged in my plucked flesh.

Bethlehem Outcast

Is there no warmth to heal me any more,
Straining to glimpse His manger, clutched by chills
Upon the lintel of the stable door;

Thawed by His breath, the oxen foul the floor,
While through my reedy bones the north wind shrills:
Is there no warmth to heal me any more?

Darkward His radiance reaches to explore
All nights but one whose shudder never stills
Upon the lintel of the stable door

Through which the gutturals of shepherds soar
In flight with singing star-bursts from the hills.
Is there no warmth to heal me any more?

Watching the magi yield Him royal store,
I wait held back and bound between two wills
Upon the lintel of the stable door.

Christ, save this wiseman without winter lore,
This bumpkin naked to the cold that kills!
Is there no warmth to heal me any more
Upon the lintel of the stable door?

A Duller Moses

I litter Heaven with myself, a wad
Of tedium tossed into it, debris
Marring the skyscape wherein nebulae
Have shuddered into worlds, which at His nod
Shiver as swiftly into ash. I doze and do not see
How on time's bramble bush impaling me
Each moment is a thorn aflame with God,
Burning within, without me night and day.
I tremble, dreaming between sleep and sleep
That He, both radiance and incendiary,
In my heart lies as on the cross He lay
(Which bed is fouler?), making my bone-heap—
Oh, monstrous miracle!—God's sanctuary.

Second Rate

With numb, invisible face
I wander up and down;
By less than half a pace
Betraying that the tune

Is pain's beneath the bandage
Pulsing, I comport
Myself to bear its bondage
As if I felt no hurt

Dealt by a blade that swerves
But halfway to the grain,
Scraping across the nerves
Thin echoes from the bone

Ebbing simply because
Today dies in tomorrow;
Yet none of nature's laws
Allays this subtler sorrow

The saints, whose wounds He honors
God rallies to their prime,
But delegates us sinners
His cold assistant, Time.

Love's Risk

FOR KATHERINE

Is there such a thing as love without faith? Doubt . . . is a
consequence of the risk of faith.—Tillich

She is elusive like the wind,
So is she fugitive like air,
Yet since you'd stifle for the want
Of breath, she'll come back, never fear.
For though you'll trap her in no fence,
Love's meshes will, but do not ask her whence.

Her heart that yields to all who ache
And scorns to bask upon its shelf
Reserves the secret by whose roots
Her heart lies hidden in itself.
None ravels out her reticence:
She's her own gift, but do not ask her whence.

She is as durable as oak,
She is resilient as a pine;
So, knock upon her as you will;
Yet he whose measure dared define
Her core would work her violence;
You'll see her soon, but do not ask her whence.

She stops by every lonely house,
Where no dark pain can scare her out;
Yet, building her a room within
Your faith, leave her a door of doubt
As risk, rare touch of excellence,
And she'll return, but do not ask her whence.

A Lesson in Detachment

She's learned to hold her gladness lightly,
Remembering when she was a child
Her fingers clenched a bird too tightly,
And its plumage, turned withered leaf,
No longer fluttered wild.

Sharper than bill or claw, her grief
Needled her palm that ached to bleed,
And could not, to assuage the grief
Pulsations of the tiny scrap
Crumpled against her need.

To prison love: a tiny snap
Of iron to be forged a band,
A toy to prove one day a trap
Destined to close without a qualm
Upon itself, her hand.

She bids her clutching five grow calm
Lest in their grip a wing might buckle
Beyond repair, and for her balm
She'll cup no joy now in her palm,
But perch it on her knuckle.

Song for a Marriage

Housed in each other's arms,
Thatched with each other's grace,
Your bodies, flint on steel
Striking out fire to fend
The cold away awhile;
With sweat for mortar, brace
Your walls against the sleet
And the rib-riddling wind.

A house, you house yourselves,
Housed, you will house another,
Scaled to a subtler blueprint
Than architects can draw—
A triple function yours
In this world's winter weather,
Oh, breathing brick and stone,
I look on you with awe.

A fig for praise that calls
Flesh a bundle of sticks,
Kindling for flame that feels
Like swallowing the sun!
Yet luxury turned labor's
No old maid's rancid mix,
But how bone-masonry
Outweighs the skeleton.

For a Christening

FOR MY FIRST NEPHEW

Like the first man to glance
Into a face and fathom
The word as welcome, dance
The common human rhythm;
Like all fish or fawn that came
At Adam's cry, or dove—
So you are what we name,
And what we name we love.

Or like the stars recorded
By shepherds who had striven
With wonder and thus worded
The wilderness of heaven,
Shy creature growing tame,
Taken from womb's dense grove—
You now are what we name
When what we name we love.

One with all precious things
Called from the dusk of death,
Rose-texture, whir of wings,
Garrisoned with our breath—
You wear its sheath of flame
Around, beneath, above
You, being what we name
For you are what we love.

One with the sacred powers
Man cradles on his tongue
During time's timeless hours
Whereon his heart is hung—

In the adoring frame
Made by our arms, you move;
For you are what we name,
And what we name we love.

In the Name of the Three in One,
More awesome still than yours,
From whence your mystery spun,
Wherein it yet endures,
Speaking, though holy shame
Would silence us, we prove
How what we love we name
How what we name we love!

Joyful Prophecy

FOR DARYL

If he is held in love,
the thin reeds of my baby's bones
are pipes for it, it hums

and chuckles from the hollows
as a flower whispers,
it ripples off him, suave

honey of the sunlight
stored for his kin, his kind, such lovely
mirrors of it, he

is tempted to hoard it in
his well where he may gaze at it,
yet held in love and gracious

he shares it with his sister;
but, lest death waste it on the wind,
love measures him for the man

who can hold its heartiness
fermented to a man's delight,
if he is held in love.

The Whooping Crane

Observe the Whooping Crane
Who still enjoys the weather
Despite his wingdom's wane—
A bird of different feather.

Less amorous advance
Than art unparagoned,
His swirling, sweeping dance
Becomes a saraband,

To which he dedicates
Devotion so austere
His most attuned of mates
Lays but an egg a year.

He counts it bliss, not bother,
That less than half a dozen
Make free to call him father
Or even claim him cousin.

Love Song for the Future

To our ruined vineyards come,
Little foxes, for your share
Of our blighted grapes, the tomb
Readied for our common lair.
Ants, we open you the cupboard;
Flee no more the heavy hand
Harmless as a vacant scabbard
Since our homes like yours are sand.

Catamounts so often hunted,
Wend your ways through town or city,
Since both you and we are haunted
By the Weird Ones with no pity.
Deer and bear we used to stalk,
We would spend our dying pains
Nestling you with mouse and hawk
Near our warmth until it wanes.

Weave across our faces, spiders,
Webwork fragile as a flower;
Welcome, serpents, subtle gliders,
For your poison fails in power.
Loathed no longer, learn your worth,
Toad and lizard, snail and eel—
Remnants of a living earth
Cancelled by a world of steel,

Whose miasmic glitter dances
Over beast's and man's sick daze
While our eyes which scorned St. Francis
Watch Isaiah's vision craze:
Ox and lion mingling breath
Eat the straw of doom; in tether
To the selfsame stake of death
Wolf and lamb lie down together.

Lullaby for a Grown Man

Laced in your shell of sleep,
Lie here secure from sorrow
And dread and need to weep
Till hatched anew tomorrow.
Returned to egg, strange bird,
When fetal slumber gathers
You to itself, unstirred
Cling to the night-hen's feathers.

I will her my own breast
So—lighter than a thought
Hovered over your nest—
Warming your nest of nought,
No wings may ever scatter
One twig of it where lingers
Your shell forespun to scatter
Between the sun's lank fingers.

In the Fullness of Time

I am heavy with my wait
Through each moment's long-drawn sigh
While my heart, my drowsy strummer
Plays my body tunes of calm.
I am somnolent with fate,
Gaze with animal's soft eye,
Take the humid strokes of summer
On a saint's extended palm.

Singled out, and one of many,
I have paid the selfsame debt
Of a princess frail for bearing
Of a field hand tumbled down.
I am common as a penny,
Costly as a coronet,
Pushed out of sight and mind and caring,
Comforted in peacock's down.

Pangs of glory soon must dig
Through my yielding bone their furrow
Depths of which can never measure
What I have to cultivate—
Whether rose or twisted twig;
To my joy or to my sorrow
Lying here past pain and pleasure,
I am heavy with my wait.

In Consolation

Do I love you? The question might be well
Rephrased. What do I love? Your face?
Suppose it twisted to a charred grimace.
Your mind? But if it turned hospital cell,
Though pity for its inmate might compel
Sick calls from time to time, I should embrace
A staring stranger whom I could not place.
So, cease demanding what I cannot tell

Till He who made you shows me where He keeps you,
And not some shadow of you I pursue
And, having found, have only flushed a wraith.
Nor am I Christ to cleave the dark that steeps you.
He loves you then, not I—Or if I do,
I love you only by an act of faith.

The Quarry

Rhyme

What are you, then, my love, my friend, my father,
My anybody-never-mine? Whose aim
Can wing you with a knowledge-bullet, tame
You long enough to term you fur or feather?
Labeled one species, you become another
Before I have pronounced your latest name.
My fingers itching after you, like flame
Melting to frost, you vanish into neither.

Face, mind, heart held in honor for your sake,
Magical creature none can ever snare,
Are but the trails you beat, the arcs you make,
Shy animal the color of the air,
Who are the air itself, the breath ashake
Among the leaves—the bird no longer there.

How Far?

How far is it to you by foot?
Ten thousand stones,
Two million grains of dust and soot,
All my bruised bones.

How far is it to you by sea?
Twelve hills and hollows
Of water, each one risking me
Gulped in salt swallows.

How far is it to you by rail?
A myriad meadows
Sweeping the window in a gale
Of golden shadows.

How far is it to you by air?
Ten thousand thunders,
Countless ice crystals set aflare
With rainbow wonders.

How far is it to you by light?
Two parted petals
Of eyelids flowering with sight
Where sunshine settles.

How far is it to you by love?
I have no notion.
For so to seek and find you prove
One selfsame motion.

Shifty Eyes

Your eyes, brown timid sparrows, rove,
Made wary of all resting places,
Yet seeking out a nest of love
Among the branches of our faces.

When you forsook a little while
Your dartings on that summer day
To rest a moment on my smile
Then of a sudden flew away,

Leaving your half-built nest all scattered
Because you felt a sunbeam prickle,
Because some shadow had you fluttered—
I did you ill to call you fickle,

You whose brief safety in the air
You barter for a brittle glance,
Who teeter on a curious stare
Requiring constant vigilance.

The Worshiper

Her eyes long hollowed out to pits for shadow,
Her cheeks sucking in darkness, forever making
A face at sorrow, phantom desperado,
Haunting as she is haunted, bent on taking
A stranglehold upon it to cry, "Look."
That we no more may scoff in answer, "Where?"—
She kneels and, shuddered down into the cloak
Of silence, rears her fragile walls from prayer
And music, candle, creed, and psalter
Where she may tell upon her beads her seven
Most dolorous mysteries. Above her altar
Stern Witnesses who one time crashed to Heaven
Out of their flesh's glory-gutted hull
Turn from her, being also pitiful.

The Tree of Silence

FOR NANCY

Upon the branches of our silence hang our words,
Half-ripened fruit.
Gone are the months of summer, gone
Beyond pursuit.
Let us leave, though pinched and wan,
The windfalls wither
Under the tree whose shade affords
No shelter either.

For when was language ever food for human yearning!
Sun-gilded rain
Mocking the sheen of golden peach,
Words only drain
Hearts of strength; let mortal speech
Make time and way
For life, the long and lonely learning
How to pray.

Hunger

The hour seized by the nape,
We meet with joy, yet grope
For speech, too soft a shape
For hunger honed on hope.

Our time together ends,
Leaving us drab and dry
As though only two winds
Had passed each other by.

So with the grace God offers,
It fades like seeds unsprung
Or the communion wafer's
Faint sweetness from the tongue.

Both moments must escape
Down the horizon's slope
Cast in their shadow shape
For hunger honed on hope.

With either moment vanished,
The grief-pressed heart might smother,
Were not each pain diminished
In mirroring the other.

Dialogue on Dire Possibilities

"Who'll wrench the rock
That breaks the flow
Of mind?" "How much
An hour?" "Oh, no!

"Love is not love
That asks a price,
For love is gift.
And sacrifice."

"Yet with what right
Have you the hope
That any heart
Can have such scope?

"Would not the shoulders
That dared take
The burden of
Your being break?"

"Yet I must empty
All this load,
Or die. Where then?"
"The deeps of God."

"What if I fail
To swing my gate
Out toward them? Or,
Of its own weight,

"If it should close
And, closed, should swell."
"What else have wise men
Meant by Hell?"

The Common Core

Each man's sorrow is an absolute
Each man's pain is a norm
No one can prove and no one refute.
Which is the blacker, coal or soot?
Which blows fiercer, gale or storm?
Each man's sorrow is an absolute.

No man's sickness has a synonym,
No man's disease has a double.
You weep for your love, I for my limbs—
Who mourns with reason? who over whims?
For, self-defined as a pebble,
No man's sickness has a synonym.

Gangrene is fire and cancer is burning.
Which one's deadlier? Toss
A coin to decide; past your discerning
Touch the heart's center, still and unturning,
That common core of the Cross;
You die of fire and I die of burning.

Old Man

My memories slip my mind as water pouring
Runs through the fingers of a child,
More briefly held, more swiftly tiring,
For I am old.

My thoughts, like children in a magic thicket,
Stumble in search as each new trail
Is lost in briars that overtake it
More densely still.

Yet children's wits are like young boughs that ripple
To pleasure you who train them, subtle
As mine are not. For theirs, how supple!
And mine, how brittle!

So that you lay as bright foil to their promise
Their clumsy gambol, graceful error,
But curse my blunder on the premise
That I, old horror,

Have veins where time goes running wild and laughs
Mocking at me who would proscribe it
In vain, addicted so to life's
Unhealthy habit.

Carmel: Impression

High over the grasp of the waters
And hard by the hawk of the gull
Echoing through gullies and gutters
Of wind down the rain's drifting wall,

Here the harpy hatches her egg
In the nest of my turrets whereon
Ever flies the flag of the fog
Against the mean eyelids of men—

How often in dreams I have spelt
Man's epitaph red in the froth
Of his blood or tasted in salt
Of this air clean tang of his death!

For his language has sullied the sheen
Of silence like the storm-eagle's croak,
And he plucks to a brittle bone
Pure fury with thought's probing beak.

My flesh, having drunk through its sponge
Far-off fetors of man's ennui,
Would vomit itself in a plunge
To the turbulent peace of the sea.

The Logic of Silence

I left my heart
By chance uncased
For any to saw
Without a qualm
When, found of you,
Its pulses raced,
Melting to music
In your palm,

Wherein it throbbed
Like waters shaking
And, wafted like foam
Upon their sweep,
My mind from stillness
Sometimes waking
Flowed into words
On back to sleep.

Now I move heavily
To that tune,
Teased with its words
Whose splintered chips
Massed by its tide
Into the bone
Deadlock love's weight
Against my lips.

Return

From what I am, to be what I am not,
To be what once I was, from plan and plot
To learn to take no thought,
I go, my God, to Thee.

With act of faith whose throes and throbs convulse
My heart as if all other acts were else
Than dyings, prayer than pulse,
I go, my God, to Thee.

On feet thread through by seams of blood and fire,
Dancing the narrow pathway, strictest wire,
As butterflies a briar,
I go, my God, to Thee.

To balance like a bird with wings aflare,
Pinned to the cross as though I merely were
Stenciled by light on air,
I go, my God, to Thee.

My spirit, trim, uncorseted from stress,
Stripping to wind and sunlight, to the grace
Of Eden's nakedness
Will go, my God, to Thee.

The Resolution

You broke Your teeth upon the question Why,
Sucking its acrid marrow dry,
Its taste of silence wry.

Like You, on quandaries ripened in the brain,
Dropped on the heart, I bruised in vain;
Poised on this point of pain,

We find no room, whether at odds like fencers,
We two, or in embrace like dancers,
For questions or for answers

Except ourselves when, I in You, for once
The query rests in the response,
The candle in its sconce.

"Though He Slay Me"

Still tell me no, my God, and tell me no
Till I repeat the syllable for a song,
Or hold it when my mouth is cracked like clay
Cold for a pebble underneath my tongue;
Or to my comfort as my father's stir
In sleep once solaced my child's heart that knew
Although he did not waken he was near,
Still tell me no, my God, still tell me no
And, opening thus the wound that will never heal
Save torn once more, as Jacob's in his thigh,
Chafed by the hand that dealt it, was made whole,
Still tell me no, my God, still tell me no
Until I hear in it only the hush
Between Good Friday's dusk and Easter Day,
The lullaby that locked his folded lash—
I lulled to a like darkness with Your no,
No, no, still no, the echo of Your yes
Distorted among the crevices and caves
Of the coiled ear which deep in its abyss
Resolves to music all Your negatives.

The Healing Light

FOR A FRIEND

You felt I would not harm you, dutiful
As I had been, yet love must strip to love.
Love must be sure and yet it cannot prove,
If it would yield us, not alone its soul,
But bait our need with its frail body, whence
We learn love's name is not expedience.

You felt I would not harm you, who remembered
How love at first was terror until it
Taught us wild children terror's opposite
And when we saw, upon love's heart we summered,
Guiltless, yet till then love must bare its side
Against the truth that love is crucified.

You felt I would not harm you, yet you trembled
A little to recall what wise men know:
That love must be a fool and dare not show
Its wisdom save as darkness and dissembled
Into the hideous riddle that is Hell
And where its children fall descend as well.

Offering: For All My Loves

This vessel take—
No chalice and no goblet,
Nothing so picturesque as a gourd
Or an oaken bucket,
But more like a rusty can
Kicked up from the dirt
Buckled and bent and warped,
Yet filled with the liquor of lightning,
The same as distilled from the flowers of children,
From the arbors of home,
From the wild grapes of martyrs, trampled for Christ,
Or as mixed with the solder of music,
With the webwax of words,
The same and no different,
Only shaped to misshapenness
In a hunk of corroded tin,
Hold me with care and decorum
For a little but not too long
Lest my jagged edge cut you,
My acrid drip scald you,
Etching a crooked shadow
On the lip of your proper love.

Conquered

Were my thoughts leashes,
they would draw me to you;
were my thoughts chains,
they would bind you to my heart;
were my thoughts kings,
they could command you.
Yet you cheat me of my anger
with your gentleness,
making my thoughts children
that sit around you,
flowers wilting and waiting
the dews of your attention.
For you do not wound my silence
with a sound,
but beyond word or act
bless me with your being.

Unnecessary

With your coming
the words I have arranged
stumble like year-old children,
my thoughts scattered
like flustered pullets.
And yet your footfall does not sway
a single leaf enough to jostle
one atom of air from another.
Indeed, my silence
summons you as well,
my need so woven into your nature
no hands pluck apart the threads,
no ear discerns my asking from your answer.
I need as much to beg
the earth to turn
or God to be.

For Instruction

Teach me some prayer
tender as you are tender when
one of my shadows mingles with one of yours and makes
an intricate weave we walk on for a moment,
gentle as you are gentle when
you humble yourself to take my kiss,
wordless as we are wordless when
a pause has fallen between us like a petal.

Comparisons

You are like roses growing,
and I with a sense for your fragrance
would be gracious as you and not rob
the air of one petal.
Still forgive me if sometimes
you are like a drink of cold water,
and I, whose thirst is an anger,
cannot get enough.
Yet you will forgive, for, remember
how once your No was so gentle
it was more like a Yes,
with your hands in my hair
making a music that only
my heart heard?
So, in the end you are like
a song I go singing.

Defense Rests

I want
a love to hold
in my hand because love
is too much for the heart to bear
alone.

Then stop
mouthing to me
"Faith and Sacraments" when
the Host feather-heavy weighs down
my soul.

So I
blaspheme! My Lord,
John's head on your breast or
Mary's lips on your feet, would you
agree?

If this
is not enough—
upon Your sweat, Your thirst,
Your nails, and nakedness I rest
my case.

My
Bones
Being
Wiser

1963

Invitation

Here is the land where children
Feel snows that never freeze,
Where a star's the reflection
Of a baby's eyes,

Where both wise men and shepherds
Measure all Heaven no smaller
Nor larger than He is
And judge a lamb is taller,

Where old and cold for proof
Would take a stone apart,
Who find a wisp of hay
Less heavy on the heart

Come near the cradle where
The Light on hay reposes,
Where hands may touch the Word
This winter warm with roses.

Precision

The leaves blow speaking
green, lithe words
in no man's language.

Although I would
translate them—better
living in silence,

letting the leaves
breathe through me all men's
in no man's language.

Hot Air

So soft my pleasure came
Upon a dream,
Iced fire and frosted flame

It was, too brief for blame.
Yet sharp to seem
So soft. My pleasure came

And went—that was its shame,
Not that, supreme,
Iced fire and frosted flame,

It bore the ancient name
Harsh hearts blaspheme.
So soft my pleasure, came

A wind and woke me tame
To that regime
Iced fire and frosted flame

Had burnt to a black frame
Before their steam.
So soft, my pleasure, came
Iced fire and frosted flame.

Reverent Impiety

I will not fast, for I have fasted longer
Than forty days and known a leaner Lent
Than can be kept with ceremonial hunger,
Since life's a lengthier season to repent
Than the brief time when spring's first winds may tease
The ashes on the brow, when bird songs intercept
The misereres chanted on our knees,
And ritual tears that I such hours have wept
Mirror a double and a muddy vision
That would not win a blessing from a priest.
Hence, purity born from my pain's precision
Refuses here to fast upon a feast,
Glutted till now on sacraments of air,
Memorials to loves that never were.

Poor Relations

Grief was your proper privilege, so awful
No one attained it, held by you alone
An honor for the likes of me unlawful
Because I had no loss to call my own
Except the losing of such trivial things
People disdained even to notice it—
A broken doll, strayed kittens, lost tin rings,
An angry playmate, or a nurse who quit.
These mattered but as matters for your scorn
Muffled in smiles or frowns, for how dare measure
Your love that died with my love never born!
And thus you taught me not to touch your treasure.
And thus, a poor relation by your bier,
I scarcely have a penny of a tear.

Heritage

I wake up early,
the day spread out before me, blank, like a sheet of paper,
and I have nothing to write
but your name.

I wake up early,
the humid air around me is a listening ear,
and I have nothing to say
but your name.

I speak it aloud,
but your name loosed from my lips is dry like a sparrow's cheep,
having little to do
with either of us.

Let me recall
how many have waked up early and found loneliness waiting
like a small beast from the woods
made a pet,

which, when it grew up,
for all that they had coaxed it with words or with work,
would turn wild again
and tear them

though it had worn
the shape of their loves. And though they might kill it, they
        wore
its pelt like a mantle
fallen upon them

from a vanishing form
after which they cried, as I cry, "My father, my father!"
But the figure had gone.
They are gone, too,

the lost and the lonely,
with Death, the dark nurse, who has dropped all their griefs in
     her pocket.
She comes so swiftly, even though
we wake up early.

Waiting

I leave my light burning
on the chance that you may come.
You have not come.
My light burns on the blackness
as an uprooted flower
floats on the water.

I sit alone waiting.
You absent, I want no other.
You have not come.
The minutes flake from the rock
of my solitude whence
I carve your face.

I leave my line open
on the chance that you may call.
You have not called.
The silence is only the sound
of my tongueless heart
crying your name.

I will not blame you.
It is not you who elect
the lapse of my pulse
for a leaf, the catch of my breath
for a shadow, my waiting
for no one at all.

Leave-Taking

You will not come for being called by all sweet names,
your lips long drifted into dust,
your breast dried to a bone,
your loins last quivered to a chill lost years ago
are hollowed honeycombs.
And so farewell
as I sit solitary in a crowd, feeling
the sharp edge unshared laughter has,
the loneliness of love endured
alone, with all the chatter stealing from me
even the silence.
And so farewell
as now tiptoe at the edge of myself,
light with drinking the wind, I sway
over the darkness of your face, dark cheek of the moon,
flower of darkness,
and no farewell.

Honest Confession

Do not wake before you will,
Do not come until you please.
Waiting for you gives me skill
In remaining at my ease.

If we never meet again
And I am not blessed by seeing
You once more, yet my life can
Be the sweeter for your being.

For at this long last I find
What's not taught by book or art:
Out of sight's not out of mind,
Out of mind is in your heart.

For I know away from me
You make music of the air
Like the solitary tree
Falling far from any ear.

Thus I boast where many another
Owned to ignorance long ago—
Till, as now we leave each other,
Tears confess I do not know.

The One Advantage

The wrestle with an angel's
No struggle with a ghost,
A ghost who can confer no names
And whose own name is lost.

Lacking a prior birth,
The second one aborts.
Old Adam cannot die without
A body to turn corpse.

You cannot walk on water
If you can't stand on stone.
You cannot speak in other tongues
Until you've learned your own.

Dodging past Yes and No,
You, therefore, can live free,
Kept hidden from both life and death
Beneath nonentity.

From an Old Maid

You come and say that it is restful here
to speak your pain into my silences,
wafting your words across them like the hair
of drowning sailors lost in churning seas.

And if I ever told you, you would laugh
to think I made your moment's reef of calm
by holding up your listless body, half
submerged in water, lightly on my palm.

Digging into my flesh with terror's claws
until the times you hope you hear the oar
of your salvation, do you never pause
to wonder when or where I drift to shore?

Complaint

Though you elude my leash of love,
my cage of care,
my net of need
so deftly that you keep your flight
a secret from yourself—
yet in your gracious circles you entwine me
whose spinning head follows your swift darting
till I fall dizzy,
caught captive in such freedom,
as the damned are trapped,
all tumbling down the bottomless abyss,
a flock of birds flying the boundless skies
of their full liberty
to go to Hell.

Love Song Minus Words and Music

For lulling this child
on the pulse of your gentleness,
too old for gentleness of your pulse;

for letting its head
lie down, if only for a moment,
within the shadow of your quietude;

for letting your words
speak to its wordlessness, your lips
improvising for it an echo—

this child whose form only
your eyes evoke is innocent
of how to insult you with thanks

save by its tears falling
into your hands like flowers withered
too long for the touch of the sun.

Warning

It was not much to do:
the flames of my sacrifice
were so small, they might have felt like a flicker of wind
in a martyr's holocaust;
my scourging so light
might have fallen, a kiss
on his bloody back,
and my cross so weightless
might have been some curious craft
flirting with flight.
Yet, unregarded, my gnat's cry, nit's clamor
shall, like Gabriel's trumpet,
shatter your diamond panes.

Hope

Is there no end at all,
riding down the rope of the wind,
winding down into the pit of the self,
falling, falling, falling
toward the bottom of darkness,
save a ledge that the foot catches on
for a moment to let me
kneel on the rushes of prayer!
Yet under my knee
the knob of earth crumbles
down the dark shaft of air
toward the underground river of sleep,
where side by side may we float
after our sweet toil together,
scarcely touching, but drifting
out toward the sunlight—
double rose on one stem!

Elusive

[handwritten: mystery]

Your heart beats under my hand like a bird,
like a bird I would hold in my hand,
yet if I could coop it there it would be you no longer
and like a most delicate bird would die.
But that music playing, those notes circling about me
like birds weaving an intricate ballet in air,
that music composed and made and heard by men who have
    never known you,
whom you do not know,
impersonal as birds and intimate as birds with themselves
(not being "he" and "she," but not being "it")—
that is most you.

Regret

[handwritten: sharp]

Had you come to me
as I to you once
with naked asking,
I should have let you.
We should have slept,
two arrows bound together
wounding no one.
Instead, you chose to lie
set to the bow of your own darkness.

Protest

Where the air in this room warms by the fire like a cat,
where music no one can touch swaddles the ear in satin,
where one may hear words as though he were tasting them,
where wine curls over the tongue, sliding down like a lover's
    kiss,
where the merest shadow of love bears the odor of roses
in whose heart I am flayed as by fire,
here I lie naked, spitted upon my senses
like a plucked bird caught upon thorns.

At a Child's Baptism

FOR SARAH ELIZABETH

Hold her softly, not for long
Love lies sleeping on your arm,
Shyer than a bird in song,
Quick to fly off in alarm.

It is well that you are wise,
Knowing she for whom you care
Is not yours as prey or prize,
No more to be owned than air.

To your wisdom you add grace,
Which will give your child release
From the ark of your embrace
That she may return with peace

Till she joins the elemental.
God Himself now holds your daughter
Softly, too, by this most gentle
Rein of all, this drop of water.

Letters to a Young Girl Considering a Religious Vocation

I

I hope that you are certain,
for if you are not, you will be
a baby playing with matches
and may burn up your whole world.
Soon you will find
that the cross is less often of wood
than of air, that the nails are the winds
whistling through the holes in your heart.
Since the cross is implied
in the shape of everybody,
do not say I presume
who wear no habit
but the habit of every day.
Where else but here have I learned
how well we do
to get through our lives alive!
So, I could wish for you
that there, where you are supposed to die,
you do not finish as merely
an extended death-gasp.
It would be a matter for weeping
were we to stand side by side
and not to be told apart
when dissected down to our cinders
that used to be souls.

II

After our applause,
harmless enough in itself,
after our envy,
not really malignant,
after our praise,
which, though it cannot carry you far,

cannot wreck you,
if you are determined to go—
may all of this cease
in a hush that is more than their echo
of a whining importunity
whereto you grimace and gesture
and writhe and gyrate
and wriggle and jump
in the postures of peace;
more than their elongation
of the shadow cast by a crone
clapping her toothless gums
stealing the name of silence.

Pilgrim Perplexed

Here in the desert of the day
or the marshes of monotony
or the flatlands of finitude
(the designation is indifferent,
because the geography is undistinguished)—
who would believe if I told him
how the air falls, a foot on my heart,
how the telephone coils, a black silent shadow,
how the light and the dark form the stripes
on the back of an invisible tiger,
crouching under the bed
and behind the tables and chairs?
Nor would anyone guess how you are my angel
here in this terrain, in this atmosphere
drunk on its very sobriety—
you, hair awry for a halo,
a cloud of dust doing for wings,
a stammering breath for a message
which you speak by a gesture
as all love speaks anyway, talking with its hands.
I myself can scarcely conceive
here where prayer is no more
than a set mouth and clenched teeth,
and every presence fleshed in an absence,
how your eyes hold reflected that vision
which is unbearable, being
the only one mortals can bear.

Witness for the Defense

Small flower turning toward the sun,
You turn to find your mother's breast.
So white, so helpless, so your own,
The Host within your hand may rest.

Hive, then, the honey of this hour
In your each cell and never wish,
When you grow wiser, that the flower
Of thought had not its roots in flesh

Whose substance caused by loving art
For a few moments more to linger
Soon melts to space, which forms its heart,
To balance on your spirit's finger.

In Love

You do not move to music,
yet in your presence sit my bones
singing in silence.
And if they sang aloud
for every one to hear
I should not care.

Sometimes on your subtlety
you wear obtuseness like a wart,
and you grow all rough edges
bruising my heart.
Yet if I catch and keep you in a tear,
I love my weeping.

Clumsy, yet most delicate
are you to take a word
and make of breath
a home, for were love not the name
of where I live, I would be nothing,
being nowhere.

Each after Its Own Kind

My weapons of words,
my battlements of breath,
my tactics of tears
I have laid aside.
I keep still
like a child
sitting upon the floor,
waiting.
I can do nothing
except acknowledge that you
are to be trusted
not to be stone and oak,
but to be wind and water,
washing both away.

Metamorphoses

You kissed her, and I watched you for a moment
bridled to your desire, tamed to the will of the woods,
to the way of the wilds, your urbane grace
skittish and shy compared to the creature come down to drink of
    her beauty by dusk.
And I thought for a moment how
my body might be other than itself—
its proper parts be banks whereon you rested,
groves wherein you sheltered, pastures where you pleasured,
my speaking be the flow and ravel of its lines
leaping, cascading, sharply declining downward,
opened into the pool of shadow wherein you dived at leisure.

And under your kiss that it could not feel
my flesh, dispassionate stick beside you, startled
back to its formal freedom.

The Perpetual Penitent

When every bright bird's song
becomes a hissing tongue,
when every leaf has laid
against his throat a blade,
when all the breezes spin
the dark yarn of his sin,
when grass shoots pins and needles
into his feet and wheedles
confessions from him, and
the air's a burning brand—
he asks from time to time
the nature of his crime,
whereon the skies, once shrill
to damn him, falling still,
their silence brings no cheer,
since he but blames his ear
for having some disease,
for which upon his knees
down life's long aisle he'll falter
toward a retreating altar
where, if by trying hard
he'd reach, his high reward
would be soon to exhaust
himself as holocaust.

Belated Lullaby

Your love and anger sweep
Into one tide of sleep
Past hearing, beyond seeing
Where you in your own being

Lulled by your own pulse beat,
Warmed by your own heart's heat—
Marry your own night, pollen
From your closed eyelids fallen,

Repose where your breath is
A coil of silences,
Recline where its release
Balances war and peace

In easy elegance
Where flesh and spirit dance,
Shadowing, bound yet free,
Bach's ordered ecstasy.

Caught in the Act

We ascertain your stone
Correctly set in place,
The grass around it mown
To an appropriate grace.

Such soft and senseless gestures
By persons of perspicience
Seemed all so many postures
For which you had no patience.

But even if you mock
We cannot catch your jeer,
And here we will come back
To you who are not here.

(Or so you'd have it said,
All tidy in your shroud,
Like a baby tucked in bed,
So proper and so proud.)

Me and Schweitzer

Little brown patches
pasted against the wall,
folded into the shadows—
moths are so fragile.

You say, "What was that?"
and it was only a moth,
fluttering whisper ticking
against a light bulb.

How can you bear to kill
one with a well-aimed newspaper
watch it fall like a leaf from a lampshade—
you as gentle as moths

crumpled upon
my pulse, rotting inside
my vein, their minute deaths
in my bone lively!

Or as Gertrude Stein Says . . .

The sky is as blue as itself,
and the tree is as green as its leaves.
How shall I write a poem about today?

The tree stands—
but the tree has no feet.
The tree leans its head—
but the tree is not tired,
growing without resting
resting without pausing.

Let me try again.

The wind blows.
How, having no whistle?
The wind sings.
How, having no tune?
The wind sighs.
How, having no heart?
Yet it is lovers who borrow
from the wind their softness and storms.

Well then, the wind moves.
How, having no body
but the motion of bodies?

When the sky is as blue as itself,
and the tree is as green as its leaves—
a poem is only
taking a child's downy skull
gently between your hands
and, with not so much breath as might startle a gnat's wing,
whispering,
"Look!"

On Receiving a Philosopher's Autograph

Your ponderousness is nimbler than our nets;
you under your absurd weight outleap
our cleverest catches, dancing elephant;
in and out of your latinities you scuttle, squirrel,
hiding your nuts of meaning, which if we found them,
our dull teeth could not crack them, which keep you alive
and lively. Under our wariest watch you change your colors,
but keep your true one secret, shrewd chameleon.
You'll not be caught nor caged, and if defined,
you'll shed the definitions as a snake its skins.
Making such names for you is blowing bubbles
which burst the instant that we touch them.
Yet if we've caught one lesson, it is this—
we do not hold the wind, the wind holds us—
or so I felt that day you turned to me
and for the moment while you signed your name
gave all your substance in your shadow.

The End and the Beginning

Not knowing your address, I write you this letter
on the blank sheet of my breath
with the invisible ink of the wind
in the script of my tears:

Not knowing where you live, I say . . .
But who knows
where anyone lives?

Therefore,

Dear Love,
We flow through one another's fingers like drops of water!
We fly through the halls of one another's hearts into the night.
Remember, my love,
how you lit on my palm for a moment
and then were gone.
And my flesh you may happen to touch is only a feather
sprinkled and spelled by the salt of a moment's magic.
Your body is fresh and as firm as an apple;
its parts that I stroke like a child fingering her rosary—
from your face which rises upon my mornings instead of the sun
and enlightens my gloom more than the moonlight
down to the bright hairs webbed dark as a secret folded upon
        itself like a flower—
are only a shadow in which you lie hidden.
My own shape is the shade of a bubble
blown till it bursts out of your sight.
My love, tell me, then,
spilling at last out of each other's hands
fluttering helplessly like the broken wings of a bird,
will God gather us up?

The Ghostly Beast

My broken bones cry out for love
To bind me tighter than a glove,
Whereas I scarcely feel your hand
Bestowing what my bones demand.

I have no origin nor end
Within your heart's deep night unpenned;
You pick me up to set me down
Where I in seas of freedom drown.

Your weight withdrawn weighs burdensome
Upon my flesh till I become
The interval between two breaths,
A life lived out in little deaths.

Your airy fingers rub me raw
More than wolf's fang or tiger's claw;
The shadows of your passing rip
Skin from my body like a whip.

Distilling dew into a wine,
You make me grosser than a swine;
You feast me on platonic fare
Until I turn into a bear.

Though my protest may be no crisper
In your dominions than a whisper,
In rhymes like catapulted stones
My love cries out for broken bones.

Evensong

"Lighten our darkness, we beseech thee, O Lord";
for it is deep, this darkness that we wake to,
or go to sleep in.
It makes small difference
whether we say this prayer
at night or in the morning.
Are the darkness and the light both alike to thee, O Lord?
So are they to us, blind moles who burrow in the dust of the air.
"And by thy great mercy defend us from all perils and dangers
      of this night,"
of this night. We are precise.
Not of the night shaken by campfire and candle.
Not of the night scared off by electric light bulb and
      fluorescence,
but of the night never touched by the sunlight,
the night that is everyman's heart,
huge vine, running wild,
whose tendrils entrap us.
"For the love of thy Son, our Savior, Jesus Christ,"
of Him, mirror of God and Man.
But of us! Alas, O Lord,
we poor ghosts stand before a mirror,
wasting the waters of our images,
pouring them into
a glass without a bottom!

Easter Eve: A Fantasy

The day does not speak above a whisper, is a high dividing
upon a moment into ebbing and flowing,
two pairs of lips neither pressing nor quite yet parting,
the twilight between sleep and waking,
the bowl of hush held lifted to the bird's first trilling.
Yet the day does not wait. It has become a waiting
as we have become our shadows stuffed full of wind and
        walking,
and if my hand reached toward you, it would pass through you.
For the world has become a dream of that sleeping Head
which on Friday we pierced and folded in dust
until He awakens tomorrow when the light of His Rising
hardens to hills and crystallizes to rocks and ripples to streams.

My Bones Being Wiser

A EUCHARISTIC MEDITATION

At Thy Word
my mind may wander,
but my bones worship
beneath the dark waters of my blood
whose scavenger fish
have picked them clean.

Upon them
Thy laws are written,
Thy days are notched,
and against the soreness of my flesh
they cry out the Creed
crossing themselves

against the cold,
huddled together,
rubbing themselves,
taking the posture of penitence,
warmed with the breath
of Thy absolution.

My eyes weep,
my heart refuses
to lift its head.
Still at Thy Comfortable Words
my bones, thrice deniers, stretch high, singing
a triple holy.

They would keep,
if not their joy
at least their sorrow
secret, but lie on Thy altar,
a bundle of faggots
ready for burning.

My flesh is
the shadow of pride
cast by my bones
at whose core lies cradled a child tender
and terrible, like
the Lamb he prays

to have mercy,
lest the hands held up
fall empty, lest
the light-as-air Host be only air.
Yet the Child within
my bones knows better.

Though the dews of
thanksgiving never
revive my mind, my heart, or my flesh—my blest bones dance
out the door with glory
worn inside out.

A Dream from the Dark Night

Not a single one of Teresa's letters to John of the Cross remains. One day he suddenly said to one of his brethren that there was still one thing to which he was attached. From a sack he brought out paper after paper covered with firm, graceful handwriting, and burned them. They were the letters of Teresa of Jesus.—Marcelle Auclair, *Teresa of Avila*

Sometimes when the silence howls in my head
till I can hear nothing else,
when it would drown out discourse and music
(were I suffered to hear them)
here in the swirling sand dunes
where the only word spoken
cries at the quick of the heart,
where images, mind's alabaster and ivory
blow away into dust—
her script as rare as a necklace of ash,
fine as a lizard's footprint,
vital as tendrils veining white walls of her cells
I remember as one sucks a stone
and so take them and burn them
while I turn to You, O my God, my bruised feet
leaping the meadows of Your flesh
to the desert of darkness
where Your silence speaks so loud
I cannot hear You.

Self-Ordained

Lithe shadows flickering across a rock
Flashed the expressions of his face, the heir
Of heretic and rebel, forged from shock
Of lust dark in some granite-tufted lair.
I watched him kneel down like a buckled rod
Over his darkness gathered in a gulf,
An upstart Jacob wrestling with his God
Or some inflated image of himself,
Or both, who knows? His words dropped blazing brands
Upon injustice, which, smoked out, still lingers.
But as he lifted proud and angry hands
I saw the victims dangling from his fingers.
Then I remembered what his Master said
Of wheat and tares, and mildly bowed my head.

Judas

Always I lay upon the brink of love,
Impotent, waiting till the waters stirred,
And no one healed my weakness with a word;
For no words healed me without words to prove
My heart, which, when the kiss of Mary wove
His shroud, my tongueless anguish spurred
To cool dissent, and which, each time I heard
John whisper to Him, moaned but could not move.

While Peter deeply drowsed within love's deep
I cramped upon its margin, glad to share
The sop Christ gave me, yet its bitter bite
Dried up my ducts. Praise Peter, who could weep
His sin away, but never see me where
I hang, huge teardrop on the cheek of night.

Bedtime Prayer

Thank you for Holy Communion this morning,
although it was the ritual I enjoy most—
the bowing at the right time, the crossing myself at the right
    place,
missing no trick—
like a child with a new toy.
Thank You that I could visit my sick friend, Frances,
though she was such a bore that I felt rather good about it
till my feeling of goodness gave me a feeling of badness
and I was tossed to and fro on the pinpricks of pride and shame
like the Christian martyrs on the Roman spears
(but they at least knew whose martyrs they were, while I wasn't
    sure).
Thank You, too, that the masks are fixed back
on the face of my love and on mine,
although for a moment we had burst through them
as from the webs of a spider.
Naked and frightened our faces stared at each other,
ugly with sticky membrane still clinging about them.
But soon we spun them once more as though we were breathing
    them out.
Finally, thank You, O Lord, that I, am so sleepy.
I thank You for this without reservation,
my need urging my gratitude, my gratitude urging my need,
ready to sink into sleep as a drowning man into water,
in whom, as both actor and audience,
his role is the real.

Spinster's Lullaby

FOR JEFF

Clinging to my breast, no stronger
Than a small snail snugly curled,
Safe a moment from the world,
Lullaby a little longer.

Wondering how one tiny human
Resting so, on toothpick knees
In my scraggly lap, gets ease,
I rejoice, no less a woman

With my nipples pinched and dumb
To your need whose one word's sucking.
Never mind, though. To my rocking
Nap a minute, find your thumb

While I gnaw a dream and nod
To the gracious sway that settles
Both our hearts, imperiled petals
Trembling on the pulse of God.

Trimming the Sails

I move among my pots and pans
That have no life except my own,
Nor warmth save from my flesh and bone,
That serve my tastes and not a man's.

I'm jealous of each plate and cup,
Frail symbol of my womanhood.
Creator-like, I call it good
And vow I will not give it up.

I move among my things and think
Of Woolman, who, for loving care
He had for slaves, used wooden ware,
And wash my silver in the sink,

Wishing my knives and forks were finer.
Though Lady Poverty won heart
Of Francis, her male counterpart
Would find in me a sad decliner.

Sometimes regret's old dogs will hound me
With feeble barks, yet my true love
Is Brother Fire and Sister Stove
And walls and friends and books around me.

Yet to renounce your high romances
Being part pain—may so to do
Prove half humility that you
May bless, good Woolman and sweet Francis!

The One Thing Needful

"The cause of loving God is God alone,
And measure of this love there should be none."
Lest Bernard take my rhyming him amiss,
I'll tell him there's no poetry but this.

Therefore, young man, as good as debonair,
Who give your Gospel with so fine a flair,
I'd not quarrel with you on a single phrase
Save to remind you what St. Bernard says.

And more, "The Love that saved us from damnation
Saved angels from the need of such salvation."
Have you, I wonder, ever understood
Love so impartial perils platitude?

You tell us that since first you yielded up
Your all to God, he's overflowed your cup.
You give, God gives—so far a game God's won.
Who, after all, outplays the Champion?

I do not hint you'd not serve God for nought,
Nor from the malice whetted on such thought
Give theologians room to theorize
That Satan is a sorehead in disguise.

I'm certain that your grief-astounded gaze,
Adjusting, would dissolve to tears of praise.
For so did Francis's in rapt communion,
St. Joan of Arc's, blunt Luther's, and poor Bunyan's.

And Job himself, though he could not approve
God's justice, could do nothing else but love
As he could not help breathing, being hungry
For air, no less so when the air turned angry.

But still the love we have no right to measure
Concerns itself with neither pain nor pleasure.
What then? St. Bernard tells us. And there is,
God knows, no rhyme nor reason except his.

Carol of Brother Ass

In the barnyard of my bone
Let the animals kneel down—
Neither ecstasy nor anger,
Wrath nor mildness need hide longer,
On the branching veins together
Dove may sing with hawk her brother.

Let the river of my blood
Turned by star to golden flood
Be the wholesome radiance
Where the subtle fish may dance,
Where the only bait to bite
Dangles from the lures of light.

Let the deep angelic strain
Pierce the hollows of my brain;
Struck for want of better bell,
Every nerve grow musical;
Make my thews and sinews hum
And my tautened skin a drum.

Bend, astonished, haughty head
Ringing with the shepherds' tread;
Heart, suspended, rib to rib,
Rock the Christ Child in your crib,
Till so hidden, Love afresh
Lovely walks the world in flesh.

Renewal

I, like a stone
kneel while the waters
of prayer wash over me.

Like a hare havened
in its own stillness
I freeze against Thy whiteness.

Once more myself,
I feed upon
Thy manna of the minutes.

Bread-and-Butter Letter Not Sent

I crawl over myself
and, looking back over my shoulder,
surveying my fallen form,
mutter, "Aha!" like a mountain climber.

Popes and silly girls have visions,
but me, lost in the desert of myself,
Christ and His holy angels
have left severely alone.

Dear friend, in the swing of the sunlight
let me hold the knowledge of my pain
far away, like the sea in a shell
and wash my wounds for awhile in sleep.

I am sorry to sing you
no more melodious song, yet only
the taste of its notes biting my tongue reminds me,
sometimes, that I am alive.

Song for a Summer Afternoon

I look from my cage of cold
that hums like some sleepy monster
at the green trees waving over the tumble-down garage.
And the mourning dove mourns with the name of my long-lost
    love.

I hear the sparrows snipping pieces out of the hush,
I hear the cicadas murmur, voice of the silence,
of loneliness, invisible thread binding the years together.
And the mourning dove mourns with the name of my long-lost
    love.

I hear upon the thresholds of their cloudy kennels
the dogs of the thunder growling deep in their throats
as they strain at the yellow leashes of lightning.
And the mourning dove mourns with the name of my long-lost
    love.

All the summer days are one day, sick-sweet with the jasmine of
    yearning,
and I have grown neither taller nor older,
but only my shadow.
And the mourning dove mourns with the name of my long-lost
    love.

Peril

My words
beat at the cage of my bones
like birds.

Its door
never opened, bright wings strew
the floor.

My cries
catch in the web of my veins
like flies.

By art
they must escape that fat spider,
my heart.

Aubade

I press against the emptiness
and pray the air into a shape
which dreams will not shore up.

I listen to my next-door neighbor
scuffling about like a dry leaf.
She once had a body

like mine that, rotting with its ripeness,
falls from the branch of morning to
sullen floor of sleep.

Resolve

I must go back to the small place,
to the swept place,
to the still place,
to the silence under the drip of the dew,
under the beat of the bird's pulse,
under the whir of the gnat's wing,
to the silence under the absence of noise,
there bathe my hands and my heart
in the hush,
there rinse my ears and my eyes,
there know Thy voice and Thy face,
until when, O my God, do I knock
with motionless knuckles
on the crystal door of the air
hung on the hinge of the wind.

Commital

You are your own best news to me; so, speak
Or do not speak—the truth of you remains.
The lines that flow between us are not chains.
Such is my faith, although my faith is weak.

Let speaking be your silence, or your silence
Be speech, I try to trust. If I confess
My faith as feeble, it is faith no less
Begging your pardon to restore the balance—

A parable that God need never prove
Himself by being what we ask or think,
And if we test His waters when we drink,
Love smiles, yet will be nothing else but Love.

Loneliness

So deep is this silence
that the insects, the birds,
the talk of the neighbors in the distance,
the whir of the traffic, the music
are only its voices
and do not contradict it.

So deep is this crying
that the silence, the hush,
the quiet, the stillness, the not speaking,
the never hearing a word
are only the surge
of its innumerable waters.

This silence, this crying,
O my God, is my country
with Yours the sole footstep besides my own.
Save me amid its landscapes
so terrible, strange
I am almost in love with them!

Thank-You Note

You give this gift to me
A gift that cannot be
For me by right or grace,
Yet one I dare embrace.

For it will signify
The truth within a lie,
A token that, from you,
I may not keep, yet do.

Origin

By the thread of her singing
the bird poises silence
that will crush her.

I myself am that bird,
loneliness that silence,
hair-hung boulder.

Upon my bird's heart whetted,
the thought of you being
the blade, cuts it.

A Bird in the Hand

I do not feel the peace of the saints,
light fusing with darkness,
passing all understanding.

Nor yet the peace of the dead, who have drifted
beyond stir and stillness,
nothing to understand.

Mine, the catching of breath after pain,
the peace of those who have
almost died and still live.

I pray that the peace of God fall upon me;
the dead's comes unprayed;
but, for now, this suffices.

Contemplative

Blackbird folding her wings,
in the shade sits a nun
cool as a shadow,

yet a lens leashing the light
through its single eye, she
kindles the leaf

of our lives to flame,
just as, stiff as a stick,
day after day

she prays, washing with words
from her clear springs of singing
a dark world white.

Love's Eschatology

I touch you all over
as if every part were a petal
when now you are away.

Never has your body
before so budded to my senses
as to my empty fingers.

Love, may we in Heaven
view all for the first time forever
through the lens of the last.

Restraint

You are like water, which is
neither cold nor hot, tasting
only of itself.

Nothing else serves but water,
cool or warm, I do not care
I am so thirsty,

like a little child
who, yet, when you come sips warily
beyond his years,

more like men of the desert
who have always to keep one swallow
ahead of drouth,

or like penitents
with their lips brushing the chalice
more lightly than moths.

Note of Apology to Medea

A fluttered-down handkerchief,
so lightly she lies on the moot point
of resting or rising.

Now she eddies about,
a leaf in her own whirling, winding
the air in her brightness.

Her paws are like petals
and, although her claws are like thorns,
she means us no ill

when she mistakes our fingers
for the mouse of tomorrow, the catch
of her innocent cunning.

Enough, if by grace of such grace,
our smiles with no elsewhere to go
light on her who, all unbeholden,

lifts us and holds us a moment
in love's loop of laughter, a child's swing
shadowing turbulent waters.

Such frailty having borne
our burden even a second, how dare we
have named her Medea!

Minor Revelation

Like you, your notes may be
All inarticulate,
Yet show you think of me,
Hence calmly I await
Their coming whose intent
Is love's rich sacrament.

Smile at me, if you choose,
That I see allegory
Which for me does not lose
By being just the story
And homely parable
A child might think to tell:

God's secrets in a sign
None parses phrase by phrase,
For neither bread nor wine
Expounds to us His ways
In ways we can discuss—
Save that He thinks of us.

So, every hour I wake
I praise God that His wrath
Tempers for me who take
To Him this humblest path,
That He, indeed, insures
His mysteries in yours.

Casual

The grief that wears me now I will wear yet
cut to a pattern with pain's shears,
sown with a fine seam of sorrow,
stitched with tears,
fitted so snugly about me with sweat
till on that morrow
never a beauty shall go more proudly
in silk or satin, velvet or furs,
and, oh, such rich-rare stuffs no old maid mind dares name,
or with the flounce and flaunt of that body of hers
proclaim
more loudly
or with more shine,
"Mine!"
By which day grief turned into my skin,
nerve-shocked, bleeding if pricked by a pin,
something to buffet, tear up, or tug at,
will be merely a matter to shrug at
instead of a garment for shame or for pride.
Then maybe I can cast it aside
like some desert devotee who at a word
from the wind strips to his crazy bones
and over the steaming stones
dances before the Lord.

Promise

Some day I will put you all in a book:
You strict, you strange, you wizened and you wild,
You whole, you unholy ones whom I took
My lessons from the times I was a child;
You rock, that my heart always shattered upon,
You, bruising as you slipped my fingers, water,
When sometimes rock melts and water turns stone
And which is which not seldom doesn't matter,
Because love forever comes toward us naked
Of every name, yet answering to any,
Or multimasked, looked wistful and wicked,
Brilliant and brooding, furious and funny.
Including me, this book, this temporal Heaven
Squaring the circle, makes it oddly even.

Decision

You will not return for my tears,
Nor come to my call,
And whether for days or for years
Does not matter at all,

Since sometimes a moment's too long,
Or a day's too short.
What measures the length of a song?
Not the clock but the heart.

Not being the first one to lean
Beyond hope and dread,
For no rain has kept the earth green
But the tears of the dead

And the quick. So comforted (dafter
Than some) for awhile
At least, I lie down on soft laughter
In the curve of a smile.

Taunt-Song

I hear you calling, but I do not come.
I cannot? Will not? A small difference.
Though once my every nerve would have been tense,
My body all an ear—when you were dumb.

I hear you call, but a great gulf appears
Between us such as angels will to fix,
Or furies, and whether Jordan or the Styx
Is but its shadow or its shadow theirs,

I do not know, but although you may shout
Me up and down the ways of the whole world,
I, hermit crab, here hidden, freed and furled
Within herself, need not go in or out.

Thorn in the Flesh

Light comes again
but sometimes
falls at crooked angles.

Now there is song,
but sometimes
the silence conducts it.

My days are full
but sometimes
only of your absence.

I have been healed,
but sometimes
still the whole heart hobbles.

Regression

Morning I walk tall
when darkness twitched from my shoulder
scampers to hide, a drowsy froglet,
snippet of night left over in the hedges.

Evenings, though, my shadow
lengthening, my shadow dwindling
to crawl inside itself and curl up tight
squirms, a damp baby in a soggy blanket.

Pilgrim Song

My love so wild and sweet like wind or flowing water,
I would pursue, and yet by running after
in all directions but pivot on one point.

My child so wild and sweet like wind or flowing water,
whose mother I am not nor yet your father,
you fly my keeping, and I freeze to chase you.

My God, so wild and sweet, like wind or flowing water,
I cannot hold in head or heart or hand,
yet seeking to, am with You three-in-one.

Note to the Reader

This book, these sheets of paper you pick up
And toss aside for being only ink—
This is soul's sweat and bile, black slag, outcrop
Of heart's New England, apples of its stone.
I loafed to write it, but, how toilingly
Prone on the earth and felt it knock
Hard on my breasts and belly, needling me
With grass for fingers, muttering, "Unlock!"
It may be luxury that wind has mussed
My skirt and blouse, to coax my body bare,
Or that my maid's the wind, my suitor's dust,
My bed and boudoir everywhere nowhere.
Yes, call it ease—but name my book's each word
What angels flask to pour before their Lord!

Acknowledgment

I walk with my head in the air.
For if I look below,
God, Thou art also there.
Lord, how far must I go
Down on my knees in likeness,
A little, of Thy meekness.

I walk with my head held all proud.
Ashamed to look shamefaced,
I cry my worth aloud,
Since God alone is graced
With lowliness, till I stumble
Over the Most High humble.

Lord, dare I crawl on my knees?
I find Thy cross thereunder,
My ease is my unease,
Thy whisper strikes with thunder
Thy poor competitor
Meek but by metaphor.

Onions
And
Roses
1968

On Opening One Eye

Dear Lord,
          forgive me if I do not wake just yet
although the air unrolls its silk
to ripple in the sunlight wavering through the milk-
gray clouds; although in the lithe grass, all stubby legs,
puppies and kittens tumble, living Easter eggs;
although the morning flows
over my eyelids shut and graceless,
dear Lord, forgive me, if I seek repose
from night, the nurse who, dark and faceless,
lays me on her dry breasts without a song.
I will wake before too long,
and over my lean and Lenten ribs
put on, more delicate than spiders' webs,
dear Lord. Your satin day,
and go my way.

The Protestant Cemetery in Florence

Exiled with you a moment on this island
Whose lushness folds the stark bones of the dead,
I envy you your breathless flight to Florence,
Till I recall that nothing's quite so simple,
That tables turned will wrench the stoutest heart.
For I remember how you in a letter
Wrote, "Father could have kept me had he loved me
More openly,"—dark secrets future doctors
Would probe for offered on your outspread palm.
And you took morphine till the day you died,
Though less than formerly, Italian sunshine
More curative in poems than in life.
You sought out conversation with the spirits,
An anodyne to heady draughts of flesh
Under whose influence you conceived a child,
A fact to scare a small Victorian girl
Of forty-some-odd years more than ghosts could.
"And I, who looked for only God, found you,"
You sonneteered to Robert, paying God
Rather a backhand compliment that even
A jealous Jehovah would not mind much,
Since Robert himself proved scarcely sufficient.
You looked behind you always, back toward death
Wherein alone you could have borne to hear
Your brother's name, love never having borne
The heavy past away. So I pronounce
Your epitaph carved from the facts which arch
Your grave, "Nothing is final. Only this."

The Descent

I have left the world of the photograph
taken a year and a heartache ago,
where contentment incarnated in sunlight
that was harsh in its heat but innocent
with hope that the next day would not be hopeless,
where my dog laughed in the Eden of her dumbness.
I have left all that behind as I go
into the bloody and furious darkness,
rotten with the skeletons of delight
tortured into despair, loud with their ghosts,
tomorrows decayed into yesterdays.
As I go down where God Himself is only
the solution to a thorny equation,
the distant disturber of twitching shadows,
I say to you what I tell my own heart,
"Goodbye, goodbye, expect me if you see me."

The Wisdom of Insecurity

There's no abiding city, no, not one.
The towers of stone and steel are fairy stories.
God will not play our games nor join our fun,
Does not give tit for tat, parade His glories.
And chance is chance, not providence dressed neat,
Credentials hidden in its wooden leg.
When the earth opens underneath our feet,
It is a waste of brain and breath to beg.
No angel intervenes but shouts that matter
Has been forever mostly full of holes.
So Simon Peter always walked on water,
Not merely when the lake waves licked his soles.
And when at last he saw he would not drown,
The shining knowledge turned him upside-down.

Interim

I play in my delight
the waters of my innocence
serene and white

as flesh and blood condense
to wind and sunlight; for awhile,
dear Lord, dispense

with rigor for a smile.
The only enemy that harrows
employs as guile

the whisperings of sparrows
for which as for her fallen daughters
the silence sorrows

and for my dreams, frail floaters
on some stray breath from Eldorado
fading away when Thy bright shadow
darkens my waters.

The Calling of the Names

I move from room to room.
No one is here to haunt my empty house
except the small dog dancing at my feet,
brown shadow of a loneliness,

which has no other name,
so like a child that cannot tell you his,
or else will not (who knows the difference?)
and sulks and will not say his prayers;

or like an old, old man
who has long since forgotten what he was
assuming that he ever knew, for he
was the demoniac whose name was Legion.

So, I have ceased to call.
No name has magic, summons not one ghost,
which never was, as quiet haunts my house,
Pan's pipe to which the small dog dances.

Beat Poem by an Academic Poet

Birds, birds, birds
burst from the trees, from a feeble beginning
like a bundle of sticks lit under a pot
crackling and sputtering
to the great gorgeous bonfire of sunrise
exploding far overhead
like a high hallelujah.

Birds! their wings
tickling my stomach instead of butterflies
wavering wanly; in bones, belly, blood, flapping,
Get up, get up,
till I do, chanting, by God and by glory
if you can't lick 'em, join 'em,
though body weeps dry tears.

On Not Making a Retreat

The nuns walk by in twos,
Lightly, in heavy shoes.
The nuns send praises thronging,
Their strong wills leashed and longing.

Their voices rise and fall
Washing against the wall
Of the world day after day
Till it has worn away.

The nuns hide like a knife
Under black robes red life,
But never by night betrayed,
Feeling now lust's bright blade

Slipped from its sturdy sheath
Of charity and faith,
Dislodged by the pulse afresh,
Burrows through bone and flesh—

I passing by, austere
As they whose home is here,
My lonely feet refuse,
Lightly, their heavy shoes.

Speculation

These streets as dull as, more familiar than
the lines in my own palm I never read
might have been strange, mysterious as
the streets of Istanbul. My neighbor who
picks up his evening paper might have proved
the object of my pensive interest
(I passed a man in Munich working in
his yard and mused how I had seen him
the first and last time—an incarnate transient).
But for the grace of genes and chromosomes
I might have walked about with different luggage
of language, skin, and heritage. I might
have come to my door and, on meeting me,
have pitied the poor creature standing there,
"How awful to be you!" and gone my way.
I still remember saying to my aunt
one time, "Why am I me?" and she supposing
that I had turned a much too youthful Job
burst into tears. Or maybe she had glimpsed
life's mundane craziness we
hid from each other in a game of rummy.

Embarrassed

Lord! Some assurance, please,
that I who kneel before this altar,
molding these few moments the shape of supplication,
am not gaping upon my own face in a mirror
all, all too clearly,
yet catwise pawing behind the glass for
the cat not there.

Yes! Grant some assurance
that I will not be blown out like
a match that has been struck against Your careless heel
to light Your mysterious purposes a little while;
that I am not
merely one more inexplicable pimple
upon the cosmos.

Why am I here if I
must pose such questions to the darkness
whence no heavenly fire consumes my offering.
No propriety of an Amen ends my prayer.
I stumble from
this wrong room while my apologies
freeze my tongue tight.

Cologne Cathedral

I came upon it stretched against the starlight,
a black lace
of stone. What need to enter and kneel down?
It said my prayers for me,

lifted in a sculptured moment of imploring
God in granite,
rock knees rooted in depths where all men
ferment their dreams in secret.

Teach marble prayers to us who know no longer
what to pray,
like this dumb worship's lovely gesture carven
from midnight's sweated dews.

For Honesty

Better the dark blasphemies of the blood
Than the oblations made of tissue paper.
You have preferred the sullen heart too holy
For hallelujahs piped upon tin whistles.

Pardon me, Lord, all my too ready praises
While I dispraised You on some easy joy,
Pompous red carpet on some glib thanksgiving.
Better Your honor bleeds upon my cobbles,

Your cry of dereliction twisted in my guts
Into reproof and rage, damning me blessed
And crossed for good against a lie, stone-sealed,
Lest I should rise, a puppet from a shoe box.

Oblation

I kneel,
my heart in my hands—
a cold fish,
a stale loaf.

What are
these among so many?
Lord, Your business
is to know.

I rise,
my body a shell
heavy with
emptiness,

You whom
worlds cannot contain
not disturbing
one pulse beat.

My bones
being boughs aflame
with Thy glory,
Lord, suffices.

To Jesus on Easter

You see the universe, as I see daylight,
opening to your heart
like fingers of a little child uncurling.

It lies to you no more than wood to blade,
nor will you tell me lies.
Only fools or cowards lie. And you are neither.

Not that I comprehend You, who are simpler
than all our words about you,
and deeper. They drop around you like dead leaves.

Yet I can trust you. You resembling me—
two eyes, two hands, two feet,
five senses and no more—will cup my being,

spilling toward nothingness, within your palm.
And when the last bridge breaks,
I shall walk on the bright span of your breath.

Message from a Burning Bush

See me, for I am as plain
as the nose on your face.
Look for me and discover
my promises abandoned houses.
Call me, and I will blow like a chill
through the holes in your heart.
Do not know I am here, and I lurk
hopelessly entangled among your echoes.
Snub me within the whirlwind of joy,
for why should you need me
when laughter's my double and life's
my identical twin?
Scorn me who scorch in the fires of your pain
where I burn to a crisp,
to a mocking cinder.
Yet be dumb at noontime and I
shall marry you like your own shadow
till no one can tell us apart,
not even ourselves.
None of your friends but increases
with your backwash of love.
You cannot even dedicate me a song, not a whisper,
unless every light breeze
bears it away.

Lullaby after Christmas

Little Child, sleep softly.
Mary's lullaby,
Worship of the shepherds,
Anthems from on high
May postpone the message:
You are born to die.

Little Child, sleep softly
To the tinkling coffer
Of the Three Kings bearing
Gifts they humbly offer
Lest the myrrh remind You
You are born to suffer.

Little Child, sleep softly.
Ass and sheep adore You,
Hoping that their breath may
Warm the way before you.
Sharper than the horns of
Oxen, nails will gore you.

Little Child, sleep softly.
Blood of babies slain
Near Your crib foreshadows
Yours in its deep stain.
Even God has right to
Peace before His pain.

Pontius Pilate Discusses the Proceedings of the Last Judgment

Unfortunate. Yet how was I to know,
appointed to preserve the Pax Romana,
that *he* was not another of these fools
whose crosses bristled on the hills like toothpicks.
And how were you to guess that the young girl
you burned one day in France for hearing Voices
was destined to be hailed as saint and genius,
not merely silly in the head from sex?
Most of her kind would be. And it's the duty
of men like us to save the world from madness.
Never mind who saves the world from sin.
For madness does the harm that we can see,
strangles the baby, sets the house on fire,
and rapes the women in the name of powers
we can't, nine times out of ten. And if
we're wrong the tenth time, why should we be blamed?
That judge, now, over there, he'll sit in honor
simply because he happened to follow the way
his nose led him to declare the fellow
who knelt barefooted at the Communion Rail
in a suburban parish a poor crazy
son-of-a-bitch. He bet on a sure thing
and won. Our gambles looked the same. We lost.
He really and truly was the Son of God?
I'm not surprised. The gods will play some joke—
and then get angry every time it works!

Thus Saith the Lord to the New Theologians

Whatever happens, God is no contender,
Whatever happens, God is on the spot.
In all the murkiness, in all the splendor
God is involved, and so says God, "So what?"

Mine were the hammers that built the Tower of Babel,
Mine the tongues muddled that made the going tough
Until it tumbled down. It's in the Bible!
If you don't see it, you don't look close enough.

For after all, did I not make the Devil?
If you agree, you're apt to lose your soul
Only because one lunge past Good and Evil
To where I am will land you in a hole.

He who bears witness of my might speaks truly,
He who denies me, lying, does not lie.
I count no one obedient, none unruly.
I do not have to. I am God Most Sly.

Bicker your brains out, I am none the poorer.
Defend, defy, call me true, untrue.
Hold dialogue, be sure that you're no surer.
Whether you win or lose, I always do.

De Profundis

O Lord, defend me when I go
Through the dark in daylight.
Be with me when I smile peaceably
though tigers tear at my guts.

Stay with me who talk to my friends
as an earless monster
winks at me; comfort me, starved and black-tongued,
though I eat at dainty tables.

Stand by when snowfalls of words melt in
deserts of my deafness.
Sustain me, though morning after morning,
I take life from You like death.

Accept me, though I give myself
like a cast-off garment
to a tramp, or like an idiot's
bouquet of onions and roses.

Sick Dog

"Man is the only animal that knows he must die."
Whoever spoke thus never saw a sick dog
baffled, bewildered,
sniffing death in the wind.

If I look like that, liquor is only
lapping my brain, yet one day I will lie staring
stupefied, stunned,
dumb before doom.

Sometimes I wonder whether the sky is God's wide gaze
embracing me as mine embraces my dog
bowed, burdened under
unendurable strangeness.

Exercise in Remembering

The day, holding its breath
under the sweltering sun,
has breathed never a sigh.

Summertime of decay,
proof of spring's false promises,
the green already fades.

How fitting this season
you lay, your life rotting in you
with the sounds in your throat

incomprehensible
to us as are the cicadas'
or ours to one another

so that I felt relief
to see your existence wrapped up
in death's lying precision,

pomp prayed and sung,
then given discreetly to
the lithe ruin of worms.

Adoration

The afternoon is beautiful and silent.
The white garage lifts like the cloudy pillar
Into the sunlight. The tree rears taller,
Its foliage ruffled like a green swan's plumage,
A sudden bird goes skimming through the sky
As noiseless as a fish swims in the sea,
When everything is far and near at once,
Remote as memory and luminous as now,
Till mind is cut adrift and like a web
Shimmering rides the heat waves up and down.
Nothing is half so tenuous as flesh,
Which, on the lightest pretext, steals away
To sleep in the cocoon of summer heat and haze,
When a jay's scream might tumble the brick wall
Next door to slide into the forests of the grass,
The afternoon so beautiful and silent.

The Oddballs

They spill like water in between the fingers,
Since we forget them once they're lost from view.
A tone of voice stays, an image lingers,
A shadow hovers. Soon these vanish too.

No one's at fault. We only stretch so far.
We're not so many minor hounds of heaven.
Leave them to God who tends to sun and star.
Our hands are full from seven to eleven.

But still they haunt us, set our memories aching
From time to time, like children pale and tragic,
Waste products of the world, blown shavings taking
Life from some baleful, accidental magic.

Lady of Leisure

Life never gave her any tasks
Lest labor should unnerve her.
People, she thought, were but the masks
Put on by life to serve her.

Existence was a blessed blur,
Time made a happy hum.
Waiting for life to wait on her,
She waited what might come,

And waited. Sure enough, one day
Life, servant born and bred,
Tripped in with death upon a tray
Like John the Baptist's head.

Bitterness

The old man coughs every morning
as if he would spit up his life
whose sputum clings to his lungs.

The dog whines, rattling her chain,
not comprehending her crime
when her occupation is to love.

The baby cries in his crib,
but can tell nobody the reason,
since grief requires no credentials.

The woman stripped from her dreams
shudders at loneliness each day
laid out for her like a dress.

The wind chimes waken to music
as if such sorrows nowhere existed,
but wind has always been callous.

For a Bereaved Father

No one can touch you
locked in the burning house of your sorrow,

where, far away,
no love or pity can lift a finger.

Jauntiness slung
over your shoulder, you have gone in,

and all the tears
of the angels cannot quench the blaze.

Wry little man,
sparse and dry as the hull of a nut,

Should He see to it,
your loss repaired would beggar the Lord.

What the Cicada Says

The cicada unwinding
his thin green string of song
tosses me a ribbon
if only I could catch it,

follow it as it leads
to a magic world where
pleasure and melancholy
merge, one river of feeling,

wherein to plunge myself,
dive down underneath waves of
flowers and foliage, splash in
fountains of yellow windfalls,

wherein, water-shrunk
to an ear, I might find
that the cicada says nothing
but my name and my home.

Sloth

Sloth is the summer sin
when the soul is smug
as a sunning cat
and hides herself beneath
the green docility
of shade, where growing fat,
smirking her innocence,
she makes my shadow seem her habitat.

For a Dog

You lie there, not sleeping,
only looking at me,
who dare not impute to you thought
and dare not deny it.

Your mystery
deeper than any thinking,
your being more brief than a breath
in man's cut-off sentence,

how should my mind plumb it?
The presumption, the effort
would be tearing a dewy web
with hands always too heavy.

If I said that you
were simply adoring
my face, you would not mind it, even
though I were mistaken,

though you would not know
how to excuse my pride
wishing I could worship, like you,
my whole heart in my eyes.

Change

I can remember
the sun as a great golden eagle
spreading its wings to my will.

Now it moves slowly,
a buzzard drifting across the sky
over the carrion earth,

or swoops, a hawk,
to seize the heart of a newborn puppy
dropped from his pain-crazy mother.

Now I give thanks
if its claws, absent-minded, release me
into some weed patch of sleep.

May Mourning January

He dwindles to the thin cry of a bone
she cannot hear for clamors of her grief.
He lies somewhere beneath her fogs of mourning,

if he lies there, instead of having been
mirrored in long-dead faces, now become
the shrunken shadow of their recognitions.

She clapped her hands and he, a poor old ghost,
jerked upright one more time for a child's whim.
His flesh, like a dry stick, flamed up, then fell,

and she cries for a plaything past repair.
Him none laments because no one remembers
the man the seasons buried years ago.

Remembering Aunt Helen

Dimly remembering how your life made
pious abstractions dance in flesh and blood
and stern negation gentle to a child—
my heart breaks into rainbows of hosannas
hovering around the memory of your head.
Remembering how somebody said, "Why, Helen
could ask me anything. I wouldn't mind."
I see that even timid hearts take courage
Under the uncondemning gaze of kindness.
Remembering how you told a little boy
who asked to buy your cat, "Honey, we don't
sell what we love," I think how most old maids'
affection for their pets is loneliness,
while yours was charity. The daily dust
your footstep stirred became a cloud of glory.
The dust I kick up irritates the nose.
What shall I do then? Shun strong drink as you did?
Read Scripture every night? Keep Sunday strictly?
Or practice with a different set of gimmicks?
Eat fish on Friday? Go to Mass each morning?
Or else fall into trances? Speak in tongues?
Remembering you, I think not. Although poets
grow beards, get drunk, and go to bed unmarried,
their imitators pull the selfsame antics
and never make it, because poems never
spring out of opium. So sanctity
changes its wardrobe at the wearer's will
not to be copied by poor little oddballs
playing their games of holy-holy-holy.
Remembering you, I weep because I find
the skirts discarded but the dancer vanished.

Delayed Gratitude

Become the friends of small things, I take
crickets and gnats for topic,
even the ant arched by my dog's armpit,
for whom I will write an epic

and thereby give him a voice which none
ever did for the ant,
even the Lord who made vocal chords,
creation somewhat aslant.

But he shall surely speak through my verses,
(you can like it or lump it)
the ant no child hears with ears still magic.
My poem shall prove his trumpet.

For he earns it, he and every other
animated caprice,
to me even their limited warfare
being a gesture of peace.

In a Land of Indistinct Seasons

Someone has opened a crystal pane
somewhere in the air
to let the summer out
and the autumn in.
But the leaves putting forth
no single scarlet tongue
are darkly green and silent
about their dying.

Dubious Advantage

Sniffing inside the box
from which her whelps have gone, poor dog,
she whines a little.

I set the box outside
so that her memories will melt
in sun and wind.

If my heart were only
a box! But I belong to man,
lone animal

that prophesies its death,
or, suckling images and shadows,
defines its dying.

Dirge in Jazz Time

FOR SOPHIE TUCKER

Her voice forever match to dry wood
Since, a girl, she sang for a crust,
Her innocence even then understood
As a subtler word for lust
As in age her wisdom would mean delight—
Red-hot Mama who is cold tonight.

Her voice in the veins of every man
Like radiant fire would glisten
Till his body, tuned ear, did nothing else than
Keep cocked to her tones and listen.
But the lilt in his bones has taken flight,
Since Red-hot Mama is cold tonight.

"One of these days you'll miss me." Oh yes,
Though they couldn't credit it then
That she who had flashed in a sequined dress
And danced in the nerves of men
Should have given them this terrible slight,
Not Red-hot Mama grown cold tonight!

Turn the spotlight off of the night-club floor.
Let the jazzmen muffle their drums
And their saxophones she will hear no more
Where winter forever numbs,
Where no one can warm her whose heart burned bright,
Where Red-hot Mama is cold tonight.

With No Strings Attached

I remember my dogs who have died,
their hairy shapes lumbering
into the fragility of death,

their wagging dumbness turned eloquent,
saying, "Think how we tutored you
in tenderness for its own sake,

no reward for kindness promised,
not even by Francis, who
bid birds praise God without saying why."

If Beauty Be in the Beholder's Eye: An Elegy

The fishing boat drifting
across the lake
like a ghost,

the little does staring
balanced like six
startled miracles,

the docile hills springing
up, up toward wildness
like Monday turned magic,

this loveliness your
locked lids diminish
by minutest arcs.

Travel Light

FOR ANNE

It would be best to travel light
Between the darkness and the light,
From light of sun to blaze of star
Wherever many mansions are
Or are not, being past our sight
Between the darkness and the light.

You kept it simple, friend most dear,
As you were told that time of year
The leaves fall like the evening rays
Shed from the golden bough of days
Shining upon us cool and clear,
Keeping it simple, friend most dear.

No, not that we have had one word
Of what no ear has ever heard—
The chime of seven seals all broken,
In austere Heaven to betoken
Our dusked hall traversed by a bird
Save that your memory brings the Word.

Meditation after a Death

The whole night sky seems to move,
but it is only the little clouds
ambling along the sky like woolly dogs.

Where shall I look for you now
when I think of the stars no longer
as silver porches to Heaven?

Where shall I part the branches of this hush
to spy you singing? Where
flies the song from the broken bird?

I call your name, but so softly
even my heart cannot hear me.
I should not like you to laugh,

even ever so gently.
Not but what you would pray, protect me,
do what you could—do all the blest dead's duties—

Nor would I pit No against Yes.
The truth is not found where platitudes clash,
but slips from their midst like Jesus.

Nor will I out of my mourning
maligning your merriment, twist
the fact of your pain into a jibe.

Yet after your unassuaged anguish of asking
I cannot, merely to solace my own,
make a cliché out of your death.

In Faith

FOR ANNE

Where none may come let roses go,
Urging the words lips cannot say.
Where heart may droop let roses blow
Over the sting and stun of day.
What heart music hide let roses show,
While faith must sleep let roses pray.

Where love sits still let roses fling
Aside the prim and proper rules.
When none dare breathe let roses sing
Defiance of all the sober schools.
While angels hang back, shivering,
Let roses rush, God's scarlet fools!

Elegy

FOR ROSA SELLS

No ghost crept in to tell me you were gone,
a ghost you would not credit anyway,
dispersing with a sniff black centuries
of Africa. (Or did—before you went
to your dark quiet, tidying up behind you
and troubling no one—did they howl around you,
sucking your breath, witch doctors hovered over
the frail sticks of your bones afire with fear,
the pale white faith fluttering from your fingers,
a handkerchief upon a hurricane?)
Only the light crept in instead of you.
I grieve, not for your death but for your life,
worked, like the flowers in your skimpy yard,
from lumpy clay. My race guilt I shrug off
as too abstract a tribute for a friend.
I view your untouched ironing with a sigh,
tug off the bed sheet you last week put on
and will no more, turning lady of leisure
lulled with this song of tired regrets as trite
as tears, as hackneyed as the human heart.

Addict

Each day I hacked out my heart
into black chips of words
until it was gone.

So, I snipped my heart from paper,
hurt in the hollow
where my real one was.

Now I sit idle, my hands
shaping wide arcs of nothing
serving as poems.

Entreaty

My thought clings to you
lest it slip away
into the darkness,

and there shiver, blind,
bone-cold, and in terror
like a lost child,

its blindness a dazzle
of the icy light,
the sterile glare

of stone, tree, and space
with me in the midst,
moth on a pin.

If, then, you should feel
a shadow's frail wing—
brush it off gently.

This Is the Way It Goes

The morning swoops to crush
Under its heavy heel
The shell of dream you wish
Had been spun out of steel.

Those ants inside the wall,
The minutes, pinch your brains
To animate your crawl
On stumps of aches and pains

Until the day has passed
Somehow, the dark piled deep
Around you when at last
You stumble into sleep.

Temporary Relief

My heart, a wintry forest,
had no sound but the leaves' crusty lips
till your foot among them made music.

My heart, a stony desert,
was barred with burning against all comers
till the spring wind of your breath sowed flowers.

My heart, a naked stranger,
crumpled broken along the roadside
till your fingers stopped its wounds bleeding.

I forbid my heart knowledge
that the silence, the drouth, and the hurt
assault me again with your going.

Ecclesiastes the Second

After a weary night of sleep,
Struggling across the jungle floor
Of dream—far better than to keep
Awake is to doze off some more.

After noon's heat subdues the birds,
Why match its fury in hot rages
Of verse and let a snarl of words
Mar the perfection of blank pages?

After an arduous day of toil
At doing nothing as an art,
A little liquor serves to oil
The creaking hinges of the heart.

After the evening sky expands
From dusk to darkness, waste no breath
Talking of love, the clock's slow hands
Will spin you fast enough toward death!

Renewal

The coming day,
the secret of a solitary bird,
becomes the common property of sparrows.

And I beneath
night's threadbare coverlet the dawn pulls back
wish his discovery had been kept hidden.

For as it is,
my heart remembers how it is the gage
measuring the gap of years between us.

Their number notched
upon my bones, my breath become once more
the wind that drags your name across my nerves.

And

And, you know, one time the roof came off
and I could see the inside
of everything and everybody,
including me

and God, and in was out and out
was in and up was down and down
was up and "Here kitty!" I told
lions and tigers

and, don't you know, they danced up and ate out
of my hand and no one else could see
they were just toms and tabbies and
I laughed and laughed

and poems sprouted out of my skin
that slap-happy time when I dreamed love growing
on trees as money doesn't and
my arm came off.

Modesty

Sweating a little, like a dewy apple,
As round and rosy, always a shade disheveled,
Of whom one thinks, "There goes somebody pleasant,
Not beautiful, of course, but with an air
Like a small tune half-forgotten."
                                    A little
Lovelier than beauty, your face revealed
Or hid the sun for me—though now no face
Does that—only the opening or closing
Of my own eyes—still if I were to see you
Passing along the street, I would come stand
Before you, arms hung limply at my sides
To say, "I love you, but it doesn't matter."

The Farm

FOR NINA AND VAL

Where peace goes whispering by,
creaks in the turning windmill,
lows in the cattle;
where the hot light stretches over the fields
like a lazy cat;
where the clouds scatter
and graze like sheep on the barren skies,
but gather no rain;
where the darkness opens its fist
spilling stars and the wind;
where love has grown quiet,
assuming the shapes
of the soil and the rock and the tree—
here in this land
let me rest, rest, rest, oh, filling my heart
full of a sweet emptiness!

Sophistication

When I was a child
I thought that it rained
all over the whole wide world at once,
but now, having grown much wiser,

I know that my neighbor
can receive a deluge,
and my scrap of earth lie here gasping
like a fish tossed onto land,

or that when it pours,
it is no monsoon
with the trees before long dripping in sunlight
all in a sweat about nothing.

On Approaching My Birthday

My mother bore me in the heat of summer
when the grass blanched under sun's hammer stroke
and the birds sang off key, panting between notes,
and the pear trees once all winged with whiteness
sagged, breaking with fruit, and only the zinnias,
like harlots, bloomed out vulgar and audacious,
and when the cicadas played all day long
their hidden harpsichords accompanying
her grief, my mother bore me, as I say,
then died shortly thereafter, no doubt
of her disgust and left me her disease
when I grew up to wither into truth.

Slump

Suddenly everything stops
as the swift blood declines
to a sluggish ooze amid a swamp.

The mind and the senses drift
upon a casual wind
blowing, petals of a shattered rose.

The body, God knows why, creeps
along, some crazy creature
half an insect, half a tumbleweed.

Only the heart lies awake,
a naked nerve, an eyeball
staring from the socket of the darkness.

Philosophy of Time

The days creep on, and, if I pit my pain
against the minutes, only crawl the slower.
Yet I recall when I'd have crammed the hours
into some cul-de-sac where none could find them,
while they rushed past me toward their dreaded end.
It is my heart, dear heart, that clocks my coming
toward you as it clocked your going from me,
time moving in us, not we in time.
For time is like an angry little beast
clawing inside us, tearing us to shreds.
No man has seen him, no pendulum's
his picture, being but a clumsy symbol,
convenient construct, handy hypothesis
to be discarded on that very day
all such constructions are—when time collapses
like an accordion whose tune is over.

Unteachable

Heart has no history
being born every morning
after yesterday did not happen.

Who chronicles a dream?
Or on what dusty shelf
is a sigh or a smile stored away?

Pain sweeps down like the wind,
pleasure like rain, both tumbling
time on top of the illiterate heart.

Fait Accompli

I sit while loneliness
Seeps slowly through my skin.
Waiting, I try to guess
Which one of us will win—

I or the gaunt black wolf
Who crouches in some lair
Of corner, cranny, shelf,
Ready to pounce and tear.

What need to ask when vein
Has felt the burning claws
Slash open so that pain
Beats where the heart once was?

Toward the End

The heat still hangs heavy,
yet is frayed at the edges
by a cool breeze.

Cicadas fall silent
in the midst of their droning
longer and longer.

Their green a worn habit,
the trees' branches droop downward,
dreaming of winter

when all of their leaves
will lie scattered beneath them,
fruit for the wind.

And I sit and wonder
whether snow will have piled
peace on my heart.

Invocation

Unwinding the spool of the morning,
the cicada spins his green song,
dream deeper than sleep's,

drawing me back through the lost years,
fumbling an invisible knob
on a hidden door,

a door I have always known waited
if I could but touch it to substance
and out of enchantment.

Cicada, cicada, fey doorman,
loop my heart in your skein till
my foot finds your lintel.

If I
Could
Sleep
Deeply
Enough
1974

Introduction to a Poetry Reading

I was born with my mod dress sewn onto my body,
stitched to my flesh,
basted into my bones.
I could never, somehow, take it all off
to wash the radical dirt out.
I even carry my own rock
hard in my mouth,
grinding it out bit by bit.
So, bear me
as I bear you,
high, in the grace of greeting.

Cycle

My body, weary traveler,
in an oasis drinks
from pools of sleep.

Its cells, all its million tongues,
lap up the dark coolness.
Never love went

more naked to bed than when
my body shrugs off
logic's gold sheath

in the black irrational,
water which one day
will drink my body.

After a Blackness

Just come up from near drowning—
I brush the water from my eyes,
blow my nose.

Better from an aesthetic
viewpoint to have finished the job.
Yet who lives by

such a windy diet? If
my mirror gives me as good as
it gets, fine!

But you do see me? You're certain?

Another Day

The day, damp bird, mopes on its branch where leaves
still cling with wizened fists above
the lawns all blanched the color of stale vomit.

The day drops dead, time's tune inside my skull
droning toward sleep when I lie down
lonely to lust's one-finger exercise.

Diary

Day gambols up to my bed like a dog
with the sunshine clenched between its teeth
and wagging a windy tail.
"Go away," I grumble and push it aside
and burrow my head under the covers
from the rump of the waking minutes.
But it is too late. The slippery quarry of sleep has vanished
down the rivers of darkness—
prey that has held me captive like some mythical wolf-child
suckled by tits of a four-footed mother.
Now being doubly orphaned, I roam here and there
searching the aisles of a half-dream, through the thickets of
     idleness,
in a lapsing of thought down a byway of silence
until light settles and fades
like froth on a glass of beer
in whose brown peace I brood, becoming
a shadow watching the shadows.

Nervous Night

Rain walks down the wind
in soft shoes,
and chortles in the deep holes of the earth.

Earth pads through my heart
on socked paws,
and chuckles from the red cave of my blood.

Blood strums through my veins,
that brisk hive,
and jabbers out the hiss and hum of atoms.

Insomniac's Prayer

I lie with my body knotted into a fist
clenching against itself,
arms doubled against my ribs,
knees crooking into a gnarl,
legs, side by side, martialed.

My sleep is a war against waking up,
my waking up is a slow raveling again into dark
when dreams jump out of my skull
like pictures in a child's pop-up book
onto paper if my luck can catch them
before they dribble away into dingy dawns.

Oh, who will unsnarl my body
into gestures of love?
Who will give my heart room
to fly free in its rickety cage?
Whose subtlety whisper apart my legs,
thrusting quick like a snake's tongue?
Who will nudge the dreams back into my head,
back into my bones, where rhyming with one another
like wind chimes,
they will make music whenever I move?

Brief Victory

At your soft word my night
shimmers a moment
in a rise of light,

and for a breath's suspense
I walk the waters
of your innocence.

My will one heartbeat lingers
a wash of sand
winnowed by your fingers.

Lying in Bed Late

As though I held a lover hard inside me
I keep the darkness locked behind my lashes
To seed my flesh with sleep, my head with dreams,
Pulsing to melody within my blood,
Making my stiff bones burgeon like green branches.
But now the tides are ebbing out of me,
Withdrawing from the coastlines of my lashes
Whose telltale dampness hints my heart elsewhere
When I go through the empty morning bruising
My shins upon the edges of the light.
Somnambulist with staring eyes, my mind
Broods on the soft black washes of those waters
Swept through me nightly and by day receding
Still echoed in the seashell of my body.

Tired

If I could
sleep deeply enough,
I might touch the eye
of dark, life.

Yet the way
I sleep, men drink salt.
Always wearier
upon waking—

I have written
these lines without book,
thumbing the thesaurus
of my bones.

Refugees

We walk through a lean land
where love goes hungry to protest
its grubby works.

We walk through a cold country,
where love strips naked, shucking off
its own sweet lies.

We walk through a shrewd snare
where love starves, gambling with its guts
as poker chips.

We walk through a harsh highland
where love drinks dwindling air and panics.
This rush of rock—!

Age of Aquarius, Age of Assassins

FOR GEORGE WALLACE

Conniver, my nonkissing cousin, bastard, my brother,
this poet bereft of heroes and slightly below
the angels, and therefore Satan's small sister salutes you
to question, Which land shall I leave now and head for what
    other?
From people committing such crimes where should I go
without sloughing the human skin in whose guise a crank shoots
    you?

When A-bombs, H-bombs, the whole alphabet of our guilt
indicts me no more than the ovens roasting the Jews,
no more than my cronies' mutual murder by inches?
You, more petty than yesterday's paper, what have we built
since one week, two weeks ago, since Adam was news,
but the House of the Shoe Fitting Best the Harder it Pinches!

Not that I with precision tools could construct the house better
than you, driving wooden pegs with your stone-headed hatchet.
For man is a chronic case regressing, improving,
regressing, twisting in bed to find a cool spot, turned bitter
when he finds the sheet burning again where his bones touch it.
Yet, there's some hope (though, by God, none to you) because
    he keeps moving.

Culture Shock

We have gone to the moon.
We have burned the hair of a goat.
We have offered the heart of a chicken
to the two-faced demon
who scratches himself in the darkness.
We have gone to the moon.

We have gone to the moon.
We have spoken to angels
of unspeakable matters
that would burn up your ears if you understood them.
And our lips are afoam with the holy spittle.
We have gone to the moon.

We have gone to the moon.
We have sat holding hands in a circle
so touching the shapes without hands
when great Uncle Hubert says he is lonesome but happy
with things that go bump in the night.
We have gone to the moon.

We have gone to the moon.
We do not go out in the days when the stars are against us.
We plan parties and journeys when the stars are right,
say Yes or say No as they direct us.
Our souls are strung up by wires to the zodiac.
We have gone to the moon.

December Afternoon

The leaves, midway in their turning,
have slumped from green into brown,
bleached of an elegant death.

Over their brittle corpses
creeps the damp flag of air,
the wind chime hanging, tear on the crone's cheek

of winter whose branches with bony fingers
clutching its scrawny body
cradles Christ close, unlikely secret.

First Snow in Ten Years

I fall awake into a vacuum
leashed from my drowsing
by a bird's startled squawk.

My thoughts nose the air like a sleepy hound.
No need to look
because my mind is snowing.

Winter Song without Music

The sky leaks rain
onto the washed-out grass.
Birds sulk on the branches
like inverted raindrops.
They will not die, not freeze
to anything
except a wet gray shiver.

Hurricane Watch

The trees have deserted us,
dogs hunkered down,
motionless, ears laid back.

The air has deserted us,
slumped like a corpse
to the pit of the lungs.

The insects have deserted us,
winged whispers muted
into timbres of terror.

Nature has deserted us,
a woman sloughing
off her body by frenzy.

Silence has deserted us,
absence of noise
less than heart's annihilation.

Faux Pas

I sat with you in a back pew when
your father died; for you, stared at so long,
would not gape at the helpless dead.

At your mother's funeral I thought to sit
in the same place beside you, decent as always
to the point of fault. Who would have guessed!

Dear friend, forgive my unaverted eyes.
But there's no back row of the mind to hide
here from the horror of your dying.

A Mourning for Miss Rose

The questions in her mind
were all brained birds
which she could not remember,
calling and screeching.

Their corpses littered her thoughts
and choked her dreams,
entangled the roots of her tongue,
stuffed her with silence.

So, when she died we scattered
the old easy answers over her coffin,
but the birds revived and flew out of her mouth
screaming their scorn.

Letter to Friends Dead and Living

You always liked death,
and no one could do
a damn thing about it.

You walked in hand
across the street with it,
lover and friend and angel

you called it. Well good,
we're seldom so lucky
as to get what we want.

II

Stay as sweet as you are
hanging loose while you strangle
in a dangle of nerve,

because old Ben Franklin,
that cool cat who said gray cats
look alike in the dark,

proclaimed, "If we do not
hang together, we shall
hang separately," so

said Pastor Bonhoeffer,
dividing the Word of Truth
raveled out to rope's end.

III

I write in a rage,
sitting in silence,
music burning my bones.

Lord God, keep my cool,
for I cannot
without freezing to death—

such singers at dark
walk down my hall,
whisper, "Wake up and feel

our ghosts by your bed
coming to stuff
your poems down your throat."

IV

We'll grow nostalgic someday
about times like these
like an old Bogart movie;

someday we'll tell all our children,
those of us who still have 'em,
how we kill off old friends

who don't do any good but
be dead set on dead ends.
Oh, yes, suicides and murders

look neat when compared to
this that is still done in
nice nuns' concentration camps.

V

Bach you liked, though you pronounced it Batch, and shiny cars
which drove you up the wall with love so mad
your mouth was dumb, stuffed full of their poetry.

Girls you liked, though few would have you, except one called
        Kitten.
You named her that. She drove you up the wall,
under and over. One day you took her with you.

She didn't want to go this time, but having cried Yes,
she creamed you with her No. So, mad with Bach,
Kitten and cars you died, poor Jew-boy, crazed with Jesus.

Short-Short

BY WAY OF AN ELEGY

He choked her with a bit of rag,
Life's stickly garden plot so long
Untended

The law filed him away; in jail,
before he died of stroke, she called him,
"I'm lonesome."

Even sparser of speech, he nodded,
stepping into the shower where
they found him.

Lament

No girl will he clothe golden in her womanhood,
moving inside her, lithe young animal.
Lament with me that he is only for the mirror
shattered into the teeth that tear his pride,
the flag of the defeated caught on brambles.

He, wholly run to flesh, becomes abstraction
to copulate with dreams and bed with shadows.
Lament with me that he buys nothing, owning
only a single sided coin, burning his pocket empty
until he dances to the sound of one hand clapping.

She who would wait for him will long lie lonely.
He passes her room to pump abandoned wells.
Lament with me that he fishes from dry gulches,
his brave rod useless, and if she hears a knocking
upon her door it is the wind's cold knuckles.

Good Counsel, Rarely Heeded

Lie still—the shy beasts
will lap the pool
of your attention,

its water be signed
with the quick scrawls
of their swift shadows.

A Wistfulness

I wish I had loved you
without knowing,
had touched your face, curious
what it was blossomed under my fingers,

like Adam—bright shapes, lions,
fawns, colts, bears,
nameless, playing around him,
oh, long before he knew he was naked.

Thanksgiving after Holy Communion

You come to me like a bird
lighting upon my palm,
nesting upon my tongue,
flying through the branches of my being
into the forest of my darkness.

Your wings have troubled my atoms,
set intangibles striking
together in crystal music
as the light flowers out of my body
as my body bloomed from the light.

Love Song for Easter Even

Just for a moment now I feel immortal.
I lie on the grass with you. Its green awash
like seaweed under water. The long flash
of sky above us, blue jay's wing. Lush chortle
of birdsong in the leaves. No noise to startle,
but only soothe me here. I have no wish
to lie here still, with the sun's flush
light on my skin this way, forever gentle.

Just for a moment—hush, love!—I have quit
the binds and bonds of the body inside matter.
My bones are supple as a baby's—look!—my flesh
finds not a single flaw, seems infinite,
like Christ, can tread the tips of the grass like water.
Yet you dart past my touch like Him, smooth fish!

High Noon

Summer unwinds itself like time's green tape
slowed down a little till the eye
may catch what other time flies by,
so we may feel its texture and its shape;
may store up the sweet sizzle in the trees,
the cicadas' antiphonal choirs
one memory's and one desire's;
hold clouds piled high in a cumulous frieze
depicting dreams against the arched blue air,
when earth falls silent in the spell
of noon's suspended syllable,
and it is finer than a feast to stare
caught in the yellow honey of the heat.
Handle most gently what one day
the heart will ache in vain to stay—
such minutes swifter than its ebbing beat.

Church in Heidelberg

You have been sleeping well six hundred years,
master and mistress, peacefully
smiling here, carved in effigy.
Even your dog smiles, snuggling at your feet,
as if he found it sweet
to have his wan, wild breath
domesticated into death.
Had you no children? Was that cause for tears?
Or were you much content to age alone
when lust had simmered down, yet stayed as good
essential as your daily food
digested into dark, to be considered like this stone
I touch now without embarrassment or riot
or envy of you for any gift save quiet.
And still you slept on while the Crusades roared
While many Masses hummed about your bed
with many *Misereres* for the dead
whose pity men had better sought instead.
Then when stern Luther howled about his Lord
of terrible mercy, still you never stirred,
but smiled away as though you kept
a joke between you while you slept.

Posthumous Letter to Thomas Merton

Unlike you who discovered solitude
To be "Forerunner of the Word of God,"
I search and find it no more than the soul's
Chafing against itself like any dog
Rubbing its mangy rump against a tree.
I might have asked you how to bridge the gap
Between our two alonenesses, between
Yours, self-elected, freely chosen, and
Mine blindly blundered into from the womb,
At first not even seen for what it was
And then, once recognized, raged at, kicked at,
And cursed. Perhaps there is a gulf between them,
The gulf dividing mind to which God is
A harmony, from mind to which God seems
The discord, shattering tidy tunes of thought,
Yet no, devout monk though you were, your God
Was not a mystery emasculated,
Poked at through barbed wire meshes of the creeds,
Led out well-groomed and curried for the faithful
To adulate from their safe vantage point.
Now that your words have smoked away to silence,
I dare not put an answer on your tongue,
As though a devotee had stuffed your mouth
With speeches that you never made. I only
Write you these lines, less poem than presumption,
Addressed in care of my bewilderment.
I ask you, self-styled marginal man,
Does not each sufferer always inhabit
The edges of the world as pioneer
To prove how much humanity can bear
And still be human, experimenter in
The bloody laboratory of our lives.
Taking and testing every pain tossed from
The pulsing cosmos, fragments we reshape,
As best as the materials allow,
To buttress God's cathedrals built from chaos?

A Sadness

I see so many drawn and tense,
taut against pain, arched in anger, flexed
with fury, faces wizened into fists.
And yet so many have been washed with love
from head to foot,
their bodies should shine golden with it.

It flows like sunshine down the skin,
like a soft spill of yellow grain,
like the dust from a crumble of rose petals,
a fabric finer than webs of wind spun
over the world.
Yet none may wear it for a garment.

Valse Triste

I am serious, sisters,
weaving my songs
with the black widow spiders'.

I am deadly, my brothers,
serious—death,
that primeval black humor.

I am joking, good mothers,
aping your clowns
with black cracks in their grins.

I am clowning, dumb fathers,
dandled in dust's
black seamy tuxedo.

Dry Season

My thoughts, mute birds on thorny boughs of silence
Sulking with drooping wings,
Moulting their feathers, maintain a breathless balance,
And not one sings.

With their bright music all the air once shimmered.
Now they are snared in hush.
The leaves where they in a green sunlight summered
Are a dead brush.

The air is sickroom still. Like a black nit
Each moment makes its climb
Up a steep pause of wind. For bitter grit
The birds eat time.

On the Examination Table

My eyes, two birds
crazily threshing
in the trap of their sockets,

my tongue, dry leaf
ready to fall
to the pit of my throat,

my breath, fragile moth
caught in a cave-in
of my gullet's tight tunnel,

my belly, overturned turtle,
stripped from the shell
of daily decorum,

my body, dull dog,
shies into terror's
mythical monster.

Spastics

They are not beautiful, young, and strong when it strikes,
but wizened in wombs like everyone else,
like monkeys,
like fish,
like worms,
creepy-crawlies from yesterday's rocks
tomorrow will step on.

Hence presidents, and most parents, don't have to worry.
No one in congress will die of it. No one else.
Don't worry.
They just
hang on,
drooling, stupid from watching too much TV,
born-that-way senile,

rarely marry, expected to make it with Jesus,
never really make it at all,
don't know how,
some can't
feed themselves,
fool with, *well*—Even some sappy saint said they
look young because pure.

Confession at a Friends' Meeting

Thoughts paddle in the floods of silence,
no single spar of sound to cling to,
except the rumble of my neighbor's belly,
the creaking of his shoes,

only my tears to serve as notes
upon the staff of unflawed air
for all the selves born, battered by
waters bearing none home.

Heart flails among those billows, washed
half away, uncentering down
in love saying itself without
a word, singing past music.

Enlightened Selfishness

A SECOND CONFESSION AT A FRIENDS' MEETING

A nail is driving me down
into my own silence.
This can't be how it's done.

Chairs scrape. Guts growl. Here, of course,
Nobody sings bad hymns.
But what if someone . . . ? Oh, well,

some meadowlark, outside, carols
making do for Bach,
who was, by the way, extremely

prolific with children and music,
theology
so much better than mandrakes.

My silence tingles, murks up
its pristine waters,
all of which only proves

it's scary, to say the least,
riding hobby horses
to death—friendly gray ones even.

Now You See Me, Now . . .

How I race
on the back of a beast
rearing high on a heatwave's footless hold!

I must fall,
I must sink, must go down,
smothered inside his red belly of rage.

The Irresistible Urge

What flies up in my face like a bird out of the grass,
clearing the coop of my caption,
why like a deer in a thicket hiding,
like a tiger among the branches crouching
where is enough to hold it here
firm in my fingers,
on the tip of my taste,
in an angle of eyesight,
an inch from my ear.
Summoned, my five senses pay court
too courteous for a question

(till the thicket trembles,
till the branches snap!).

Sow's Ear

I turn my life over and over
like a toy windmill or a doll.
From whatever angle I view it,
I find my death.

I measure it, weigh it, and try it.
Yet its molecules and atoms
will not add up to anything
except my death.

I may fling it over my shoulder
like a sweater almost forgotten.
Still I feel it tugged by each breeze
cold from my death.

Nobody would care except me.
Why even I should, who can say—
delicate monster, its edges
frayed toward my death!

Fantasia

Last night I lay writing a poem,
lifting barely a finger.
I did not need to.

You did it for me, my dear,
typing on me with your
invisible teeth.

I've counted your phrases, one
on my forehead and cheeks,
two on my mouth,

three on my breasts and my belly,
printing my mons veneris,
touching those places,

shadows, privates, genitals,
gentlest now if my fists
open with poems.

You with your long dusty hair
draping my shoulders, hiding
what does not need

any longer to be hidden.
Read my face and my hands
stripped raw like Jesus.

Wraith of my dead mother coming
down the hallways of midnight
with the dishcloth

she slapped my father with once,
Veronica of the Kitchen.
Never be shocked—

Only the book-ghosts can scare us,
not the real ones, their footsteps
crooked and lurching.

Impasse

Nothing moves.
Barefooted, my mind, walks over the facts.
Blind, bruise your fingers on the Braille of what is,
though, deaf, you do not know how to name it.

Yet patience. Sit down on the cold cushion of stillness.
Peer down your own depths where you hope to see something—
a face or at least a form that urges you forward—
unless with a sigh you get up, deciding
that walking alone is better than waiting out nothing.

Your soft soles and your fingers keep bleeding
as you gum your prayers, a mouth minus speech.

Nothing moves.

Minor Miner

One time
the poems lay loose like gold nuggets
spilling out of the pores of my skin.

Now I
hurtle down shafts of myself,
having become an abandoned mine,

where in
the dark, I, my lamp long gone out,
wait for the welding of rock with my bone.

Breakthrough

Come back, my cool confusion,
my dear disorientation,
my lovely Lily of the Valley,
who doesn't know she's doomed,
or simply lacks illusion
with such a clean elation
no black alarm can rally
her homeless spirit homed.

Then let's all hold communion
instead of confrontation,
you Marys, Margarets, Megs,
you mothers, sisters, daughters;
it's family reunion
that finds by acclamation
we're sick of treading eggs.
More fun to walk deep waters!

Small
Change
1976

Entry for a Summer Day

Sleep skids upon
sweaty sheets; day,
loaded gun, goes off

splattering light
and shadow while
past murky panes

the air's awash
with cicadas
and heat's high whine.

Transmogrification

I am rooted
into rocks that lie
in cool absolutes of sleep.

I stare puzzling
over the difference
between my feet and this earth.

I drowse
in the brute ambience
of clods and sticks and mould,

inverted moons
drawing down under
tides of my blood.

Any farewell messages of mine
you cannot tell
from fallen leaves.

Zen Meditation

Sit counting the breaths—
one two three four
one two Over and over—
Unriddling no conundrums,
bending the mind till it breaks in beliefs,
no tearing the heart's bloody petals—
He loves me He loves me not
Nothing matters except the little important—
one two three four
one two three four
clink clank this small change of being.

Encounter

I was content with the pseudonym
of my own name, with the disguise
provided by my body,

snapped to when anybody called me,
answered to the image captured in
eyesight's polaroid

posted for all the curious who passed,
lived, a stranger in my own skin,
because my friends defined me,

till at your word, I, somnambulist,
awakened astonished in the streets
of my identity,

and there you left me, but not before
your flesh, breathed in a muted sentence,
instructed me in mine.

The Darkness at Noonday

The day is a clear blue eye
staring straight through you

into a crystal solitude,
an azure silence,

where, if you stretch out your hands,
you will fade away at your fingertips,

the vibrating wire of your scream
disappear in sun-dazzle,

consuming your rickety dance
on the human hairsbreadth of light.

Memento Mori

IN MEMORY OF ANNE SEXTON

You think that I am smiling,
but I'm practicing my death-grin.
I must wear it for a rather long time.

You think that I am sleeping,
but I'm developing my grave skills
for when I must do death's motionless ballet.

You think that I am breathing,
but I'm toning up my death-gasp.
I owe it to my friends to do one thing right.

You think that I am resting,
but I'm hunched over my decay,
which makes do for the pretty baby I wasn't.

Indigo Ending

Green saws of the cicadas
having subsided
into a desperate rasp,

the hours hover silent,
fragile convalescents
rinsed down to bone

purified of longing,
waiting for health
as if it might be death—

the blue day being
no more than
a suspended sigh.

Since No One Will Sing Me a Lullaby . . .

Wind, mad granny,
rocking on darkness,
the tree branches your knitting needles,

knit me a blanket
from sleep's wool
made to snag on the corner of waking.

An Athenian Reminisces

Yes, I remember Paul, his ugly face
Alive with joy, his stooping shoulders seeming
Straighter somehow as if his words had driven
A rod of iron down his spine. "My friends,
The Unknown God to whom you rear an altar
I now declare!" So, he proceeded to
Domesticate the Mystery. He's dead
You say, beheaded by that madman Nero.
No doubt he scarcely felt the blade strike through
The bone so padded was he with conviction.
Courageous man! Yet now that I am old
I'm not so sure that one can be as sure
As Paul. At any rate, I've never caught
The Unknown God at leisure in His rooms.
Nor spied Him in the middle of His labors,
Although my bruise-bewildered brain would like to.
Whether or not He makes the crooked paths straight,
I've had to hack mine out as sorry-best
I might. Christ died for us, Paul taught? How strange
A god should think a man's requirements so
Excessive. All that I need is space,
Not so much larger, really, than a cat's
[Or so a deity might measure it]
To ease my cramped limbs in the sun a little.
Well, well, the names of God are beautiful—
Zeus, Hera, Demeter, Mithra, Astarte,
Isis, now Father, Son, and Holy Ghost—
So many screens behind which he eludes us.
And though stout-hearted Pauls may claim the Quarry,
Pet of their pieties, they may as well
Drag home with them a shadow by the neck.

Old Dog

Your shadow
is death, old dog,
yet you lie down beside it

as trusting
as a young pup
sleeping beside its mother

or maybe
a kindly master
gentling your exuberance,

but slowly,
lest he should scare you
wagging your tail: a spark

from sun
and moon and all
the stars love nudges onward.

Homecoming Blues

The ashes have waited for me in the ash tray,
but say nothing.
The towel hanging on the rack that I have longed to see
somehow says nothing.
My dogs who have already forgotten how much they missed me
say nothing either.
    And O O O O
I wish I could call my mother
or eat death like candy.

Accepting

Lord, serene on your symbol,
you plant your flag
on pain's last outpost.

Your arms span its horizons,
your feet explore it,
your eyes are its seas.

You, pioneer in pain,
reclaim its wastes,
and so you prove it

no more an alien planet,
only our earth
whose soil stains your fingers.

Against your side woe's wildness
strings its red vine
and shadows your face.

Then name this bloody ground
firm underfoot
home, however homely.

Raison d'Etre

I grow from my poems
in a green world.

Outside them I suck by breath,
grow pale and poor.

For I am the toad
in my imagined garden.

Light Reading

Spies whisper through my air condition units.
My drainpipes crawl with wraiths of Jack the Ripper.
A time bomb in my oven ticks off minutes,
Imperiling beans and porkchops for my dinner.
An ex-con feeds my watchdogs poison candy
And saws my burglar bars in half. My lodgers
Are little men from Mars named Rick and Randy
Cloned from the brave Flash Gordon and Buck Rogers.
Bats breed inside my breakfast room and kitchen,
Where paranoid pygmies plot their crimes.
My hundred-watt bulbs are hung with lichen.
A ghost squats on my toilet. Between times,
If things grow dull, old Nazi bombers strafe.
So, ringed with ghouls and corpses, I am safe.

Coming Home

I quit waiting up for myself,
slop over into a burp and a yawn,
kick my sense of adventure under the bed,
and curl up in yesterday's shape.

I put my smile back in the garage,
hang up my manners in the closet,
tell my sobriety to take it easy,
and tuck my memories under the pile-up of newspapers.

I take my temper out of the freezer,
warm up bad habits in the oven,
put the left-overs of my brain on ice,
and work my life back into its old shoes.

Listening to Rain at Night

Since water lacks lexicons,
rain refuses translation,
try as I may to render it—

crouching low at the passage
where sound peels away from silence,
a cleavage no mind can perceive;

crawling between heartbeat and heartbeat
after that nice precision,
shimmering language of liquid:

None shapes a goblet of words
from which you can hope to sip
the delicate racket of rain.

Approaching
Nada
1977

Approaching Nada

I

Here where these white-headed trees
blanched by the cold desert sun
open upon rosy rock
nippled and cocked toward the sky
stabbing my eye with its gaze.

Here where the land takes both breasts
gripping them firm in its palm,
guitarist of horny fingers,
playing them hard till they hurt
out of their shattering strings.

Here, where all rivers run sand,
this taking-off pad to deep space,
the air too thin for my lungs,
the water too scant for my mouth,
the gold light too rich for my flesh,
hungry for flabbier fare
than even the loaf and the wine
served sparsely on every Lord's Day,
hungry for dust on my dust
slightly more damp than the tomb's.
My Lord and my Christ, dare I come
here where the sun shrieks Thy name,
here where the wind rasps hosannas
in atonal chords on my ears,
asking the giftings of grace
sealed with these fire-signs of death!

II

One might become Quaker
in this Aztec land
where Christ is mostly Catholic
(Roman, properly), ripe in purples of his flesh and blood,
in this patio,
flooring at least gray,

the walls dulled to mustard yellow,
with the little wind chimes hushing their lascivious tinkle,
the tortoise-shell kitten
darting feather-footed
at dream-prey (favor, though small)
another sound suddenly anonymous this afternoon;
except for the sun
softly pawing my belly
parting my blouse from my trousers, so
letting my handiest fancies have all their way willy-nilly.

III

Many words do not compose the Word,
nor do our dumbnesses make up the Silence
whence Your Almighty Word leapt down
"when night was in the midst of her still course . . .
Alleluia!"

Somewhere between silence and ceremony springs the Word,
the wellhead of all hush feeding the roots
of tongues, whether of men or angels, interchange
between us and Your world. Listen, whoever
tunes an ear.

Sweet bird of Christmas singing all night long,
Hamlet in part believed as I do wholly
out of faith furnaced, fired by doubt,
wings clipped by busy book and body, still, in You,
my Phoenix!

IV

Abbé Bremond, you wrote,
"Le poète, c'est un mystique manqué."
An aborted mystic,
a frustrated mystic,
or did you mean,
simply, a sorry one?
Doubtless the latter, since

the poet like the mouse will scuttle
clean to the border
of the ineffable,
then scurry back
with tidbits of the Vision.
Whereas Juan de la Cruz,
say, or Theresa de Ávila
leaps once and for all
headlong into darkness,
drowning in dumbness,
dying Shakespearean lovers.
Mon seigneur, I wonder—
Christ's Gospel spelled these self-same saints,
"Go tell. What's whispered in your closets
shout from your rooftops.
Follow me who flaunt
my body's banner
crimson before the bulls."

These poets of the Nada
obeyed Him. So poets, mystics of
the bruising thing
climb up bloody concretes
to leave nailed high
white pieces of themselves.

                            v

Although I wander
down hallways of my body, ghost
prowling passages of my blood
to my most hidden corners, still
I know my name.
I trace footprints
of princes, rebels, martyrs,
even one poet, the last subsuming
all the rest, including—mind you—
wild Indians.

My great-grandfather,
Southern Abolitionist,
escaped a hanging aided by prayer, huffing
and puffing to loose a floor log.
When he met his captor
later that week,
each tipped his hat to the other,
going his way of crazy cordiality.
(Much talk of killing passed back home,
but little murder.)

It was exciting,
recalling Huguenots,
home-loving French folk, snubbed home for God.
I, who quake in travel bureaus,
would pray your pardons,
unsainted saints,
who seeded Louisiana
with slaves. Her ex-boy, old Hans, tramped miles
to see my grandmother, marveling
her sons could read.
My father also
told me how his father,
stern German, devout Catholic, and builder
of two churches once turned his back
upon his Bishop.
Gentler Vannah, sister
to my own mother, depicted Sherman
slashing drapes in Georgia, where Lanier
droops cattywampus on our tree
with such-like freaks
and skeletons, rattled
by chancy breezes, a tree rooted
but in God's chancy hand. Middling-good ghost.
I seek my roots of shifted waters
shifting toward Nada.

Struggling
  To
    Swim
      On
        Concrete
        1984

Admission

IN MY FATHER'S MEMORY

Wrongheaded you might have been, but you'd forebear
With me for anything and like my skin
Wrap me around, though I might squirm and swear
To get away as drunks from boozy sin.
But we were stuck together and no doubt
Your love would do for parables Christ told.
Burr in my hide, knives could not dig you out
Where you lay snuggled in its deepest fold.
I might have been served better if they could,
Poor irritation, love's persistent fly.
Yet suaver loves than yours have not withstood
My fury and neglect, have shrugged me by.
You were my absolute, if such there lives
Within the prison of the relatives.

On a Weekend in September

Come God
be man woman child old one
bread breast of the world and water
for that matter
lamb stretched down and down down to the meanest grub
struggling to swim on concrete

merged into mortal stuff
Ancient of Days of Seas
mirroring
hauled to your hard wood
Creator brought to creature

here where I remember Lee Palmer
who 80-odd years ago
prayed by no book but that terrible book of the deeps
on a weekend in September
I quickly skimmed

> *Dear Jesus*
> *make the waters recede*
> *and give us a pleasant day tomorrow to play*
> *and save my little dog Youno*

nobody remembers Lee Palmer now
why would they
he would be an old man now
dying maybe senile maybe
nobody would like him and would wish to hell he'd hurry

still I hope
Lee Palmer
swept out from Galveston in 1900
was swept up to you on the Gulf's gray tongue

because were one lapped
and lulled in the very body of the beloved
that were not bedding deep enough for one to know
and be known back

when each should tremble
cradled in the other's memory
shifting
such risky ocean

Open Sea
whose sides
eye cannot touch

For a Senile Woman

Time winds you slowly backward to the green
Of infancy, to your original
Blank, spool spilling its threads across a table.
You loose your hold on memory and thought.
Language eludes you. Almost not heard or seen,
Threads spill, your spinner's hands no longer certain.

A shape the water stirs up from its certain
Outline, you slip my grasp, your vibrant green
Washed out forever like a volume seen
Brilliant no longer, and original,
But hackneyed as a much repeated thought.
I cannot wait to brush you from my table.

You seem a shadow cast across my table,
Glimpsed from the corner of my eye not certain
That you are real and worthy of my thought
Except as reed to be uprooted, green
Trespasser on my lawn's original
Elegance and despised as soon as seen.

But you, a Thou, demand that you be seen,
Whether as fly or flower on my table.
Your withering is still original
To you, your dying struck upon me certain
As mine will strike, since black, as true as green,
Will not be banished with my wand of thought.

And if I hide from you behind a thought,
The fire of you will scorch me till I've seen
Ebbing reality is yet as green
As new creation is. I cannot table
The fact of you, homely and certain—
You in your rancid flesh original,

Yet common, Adam's share, original,
Grace and curse, both past my human thought,
Marked by Christ's birth and death, that stamp of certain
Value, thus ransomed from life's discard table,
You in your dying stay like summer, seen
Repeated never and so ever green.

Be green, old mother, my original
Claim at God's table, my best thought
That God affirms my being seen and certain.

Mistaken

I thought all that behind me—sleepless nights
With poems racing through my head like children,
Small innocence at first blush turned such frights,
Setting my brain to boil, black witch's caldron;
Each dream had heretofore kept strictest order
And, paper-trained, perched where I wanted it,
Passion itself a temporary boarder
Amusing me awhile with graceful wit,
Where even God might exercise due tact
Minding my spirit circumspect, demure
As a rinsed sand-dollar. Now my world's been cracked,
My being but an aching aperture
Naked to earth no inch of which I own,
My self my one possession held on loan.

A Rage for Order for Rose

From my back porch I'm watching God's housekeeping
And think you wouldn't want Him in your house:
No Lordy! Like them mens, no good at sweeping,
And look, just will you, all those leaves fly loose!
That great big broom God makes those old fall winds with
Like He ain't thought about nobody's yard.
Those clouds! Not fit to dry your hands with,
No wonder you could slap a tree trunk hard!
And, say, don't tell you how God wastes some comet,
And spends a million years on one amoeba
When you could—Lord, have mercy ain't no limit—
You go and close your window—just how He be.
And now, be-hold! God gets Hisself a few
Dobabs all throwed around
                          and dear like you.

After a Brief Visit

Too late too little (every moment is
Because we have to die) and yet it made
Lively once more to memory how it was
That young and yearning period I prayed
And pondered were you mother, lover, idol,
Not thinking how such puzzlement might end,
Dared not suppose, so cheaply did I peddle
Myself, or else so dearly, you were friend,
No more, no less, with the melodious mix
Of good, bad, and indifferent to embrace,
A prize to ease our spirits, not perplex:
The moderate is gift enough and grace,
Like all grace lapsing in that frail flame, breath,
When every thing affirms us, even death.

Whitewash of Houston

Who would have thought of her as mother small
town raunchy with cowhands coming and country
girls and boys not knowing Dr. Freud but
Moses very well as big-nosed Bach pumped both
organ and wife scattering music even
more than her cattle safely graze those meadows
of midnight and darknesses presences surrounding
her with cloud by day and night also going
before her where she only stumbles in
imagination fearing that they are
only dry holes reverberating with
some ancient terror tutored by none
but teachers' voices like a piece of chalk
scratched white across the face of midnight breaking?
Who would have thought of her as mother sleek
big-butted like black cars that bulging slickly
swim over pavement and pothole splattered with
delicate bone and gut of squirrel none
except poor folk afoot or else on bike
would ever notice much less mourn on grounds
as female as the moon her sons tromped on
galumping ghosts crumpling that most dainty
fingernail of poetry into a
fist fondling their rod that flaunts their flag
dribbling oil and slime and muck that ooze
from under her armpits as she stuffs her mouth
with garbage drooled onto her front until
she drops dead in her tracks to bed hot for
that prick and prong of sleep's sweet long and hard?
Who would have thought of her as mother gunning
down eerie corridors of her dark self
dented and bent the shape of truth no meaning
can measure and that has no end but life
to cradle whether for its good or ill
nobody knows however life may teem

with fact outwearing pint-sized brains made all
she ought to stand up straight behind her shame
before the world that tossed her to the dogs
as innocent as she once seemed with knowing
what shadow loops its coil about her legs
quickened with light and slowed to dusk on seeing
her terror driving all her children dumb
down the long chute of death and safely home?

II

Who would have thought of her as mother mad
at morning and mad with mourning and merry
as the scissor grinder's whistle blown far dodging
February currents and her memories
bouncing it up and down like a fey bell on
her ears as keen as gray chill cuts and leaner
than Lent has stripped away the clover blossoms
long ago vanished with the honey bees
that horny fingers of the rain uncoiled
March and April meandering across
the vacant lot of Easter and back home?
Who would have thought of her as mother fed
and fudged till fattened on her lentil vigils
as open as her covert cesspools ripe
with the rich grain of avarice and April's
froth of green and dogwood's lace hung over
the land and greening all her lawns until
she lies down with her apron smelling of summer?
Who would have thought of her as mother light
could lift into corn cribs to lie until
curious as a calf she grows and swells
with moonstruck offspring pushing all awry
who have not known the hollow of her womb
more hollow than the opening leading to it
to gobble down her shacks and spires till time
has hulled them all like winter's dried pecans
dropped to her earth leaning and lurching fawnwise
mulched with the sunshine long since loamed with darkness?

Prayer upon Waking

Give me, my God, this day
the simple human grace
and fortitude to face
my loneliness, small stray,
no wolf, no tiger,
no lion of ferocious roar,
no demon eager
for souls this at my door.
Only a little child
crying and lost, half wild
to be let in and listened to,
closer than my own kin,
she is my own,
and the sole creature who
tells me the truth so rendering You
what children by their nature do,
what long ago that stone,
my heart, was duty-bound to raise—
Your perfect praise.

No Going Away Gift

FOR JENNY AND GEORGE

Dry throat of summer rasping with cicadas—
I pace dull shops of my imagination
seeking some proper gift for you, good friends,

in vain. Besides, the pockets of my mind
would be too poor to pay enough for any,
or else my heart would lack the heart to buy it,

because my gifts are selfish celebrations,
not meant for now when custom's easy chime
sounds strange when jangled by this wind of parting.

Yet, please forgive me, since the purest gift
is relative, and love, an absolute,
must ever in the end come empty-handed.

Meditation

Ah, oh, om, ha, ho, home, go home, old
woman where there is no home—where no
one is home where all are home where every
one is home, come home when no one seems
at home, when every one seems gone,
run to a hole in the ground, hum, ho and
hum, hum ah, om, ho, home, till some
small dog summons to corporal works of mercy.

Birthday Card to Myself

Let me shrug off the sleeves of my history,
slip from the coat of my past,
snag a pinhole in the mesh of my minutes,
and, fatherless as the leaves,
tracing my lineage from the atoms—
join the mute ceremony of stones,
the speechless celebrations of grasses,
take off my name long enough
to steal by this day barefoot.

Mrs. Lot

There has to be something said for Lot's
wife, for looking back, not moving on, for,
in other words, nostalgia, that onetwo
threefourfivesixseveneightnine letter
dirty word, when even Jesus for whom
she serves as reminder says to remember
her, and why else if he didn't mean what
he said, understanding, of course, women
apt to cling to their homes, not having
in those days much else to cling to—and
what if they clung—like Lot's poor wife whose
name we don't even know to recall, she
having to pull up stakes and get out
just because some men liked other men, that
being none of her affair, besides which
she'd never liked Uncle Abraham's loose
foot she swore he was born with, and so
she has long gazed back on her past which she
couldn't put back any more than a pulled
tooth, for which crime she stands changed to a briny
pillar, still turned toward her yesterdays and
her God who surrounds her on all sides—right,
left, front, and back—her sad but salty stare.

Bagatelle

FOR HELEN GREVE

Of all the days dropped in time's pocket
this day will seek acknowledgment
with a child's shy asking,

because the love between us used
no word uncommoner than coffee,
and was never traced

by graphs of huge emotion. Yet
some fancy will recall this day
hallowed past recognition.

On Hanukkah

FOR MAXINE AND JOE

Small Jewish girl
reared in a Catholic city
you need not envy us our Christmases

outside our lighted windows
you who mostly observe
keep your festivals

for we are sad in our celebrations
mean with our merriments
uprooted from our families

dissecting our darkness
where Jesus sways
not on his tree but ours

here where he dangles
a little lower than his hosts
plastic and blinking

not red-robed as the Romans dressed him
still longer kept therefor
all of us who now light candles.

A Consolation

I long to stroke the sorrow from you,
but even had I such a healing,
you might not take it.

Love sometimes has so frail a balance,
a hair would be a warlock's wand
to witch it clumsy.

And thus, I stand aside and watch you
from across love's chasm, narrow,
never to be bridged.

I take a fragile comfort, knowing
love speaks, but also keeps a finger
upon our lips.

Morning Person

God, best at making in the morning, tossed
stars and planets, singing and dancing, rolled
Saturn's rings spinning and humming, twirled the earth
so hard it coughed and spat the moon up, brilliant
bubble floating around it for good, stretched holy
hands till birds in nervous sparks flew forth from
them and beasts—lizards, big and little, apes,
lions, elephants, dogs and cats cavorting,
tumbling over themselves, dizzy with joy when
God made us in the morning too, both man
and woman, leaving Adam no time for
sleep so nimbly was Eve bouncing out of
his side till as night came everything and
everybody, growing tired, declined, sat
down in one soft descended Hallelujah.

For a Spiritual Mentor

TO DOROTHY RICHARDSON

May I become what you are, full of years,
Robust with time, nourished on many days.
Welcoming laughter, making room for tears,
Accommodating love and anger, blame and praise:
May I become what you are, easy with
Existence and what shape it may assume—
A landscape wild and terrible as myth,
A scene as quiet as a firelit room:
May I not be like those who spit out life
Because they loathe the taste, the smell, the muss
Of happiness mixed with the herb of grief;
May I become what you are, generous
Even toward death, that is, if death could find
More than your pinch of dust unspent behind.

No Hiding Place

Naked, I swim the seas of glare,
drunk on sobriety,
delirious with clear-headedness,
stunned upon abstinence,
numb from nothing but daylight.
I meander in strict steps,
confused by the straight and narrow:
My whole life shatters
its ground glass slicing through me.
All my deaths have sharp edges.

Haunt

Never mine
in the most harmless sense,
now you are no one's

moving free
in death, state without strings.
Are these what you seek

these long nights,
malcontent, in your plot
dug dark in my mind?

Seasonal Change

I have been out of the weather of love
So many years that I barely remember
The way its winds feel, how they push and shove
Me from side to side. Accustomed to lumber
In the thick air of calm, I'm less than sure
I like this stir. I have built a home
On my edge of existence, braced secure
With waking and sleep, every door dumb
To the world outside, all windows tight shut
Like crying mouths fallen silent long since.
My heart snug and smug as a dried up nut
Blown to a cranny, its fibers wince
With this seasonal change, slow to unlearn
The temperate climate of unconcern.

Improvisation

Death we can manage,
mincing along
bearing our black bows of condolence.

But this our mind
can scarcely handle,
too heavy even for our tongues

lacking decorum
to shape this rawness
which must make up its own words.

Assertion

I am no scholar in the ways of love,
Nor skilled in, except as mind's pale structure
Patterned after some bookish architecture,
Nor have I often practiced how to move
This way or that, beneath, around, above,
Having found wanting each pedantic lecture,
Each stew of hearsay but a sorry mixture
Of curiosities I could not prove
Granted my interest—yet having ample
Wit for firm flesh, its sinewy strategem
Of eye and ear, of nose and mouth, am ready
To taste your weary sweat, to take the simple
Test of your pulse with mine, kiss your sweet stem
So bearing off the prizes in such study!

A Gift for God

You die without fear
secret-
minded like a bull,
with all your questions now
candles blown out
smoking to wisps
so high
you cannot see them—
Go wild old woman
crazy I'm not God
to save you even if
you asked.
I can only love you.

Affinity

FOR FLANNERY O'CONNOR

Fearing the city whose knife-narrow buildings
crowd sun and stars, mocking at hill and tree
fit only for the birds, and making geldings
of country heads stuffed full of piety,
you went home sick as well one might when still
the too long summers of a childhood rage
too long, faith turned a digit of the will.
Yet had Grace struck, like mumps in the middle age
to shake you loose and tell law where to go.
Or had disease and early death not shut
your door, you might have left the family pew,
thumbing your nose at every holy "Tut!"
matching strict steps to those that weave and falter,
danced David's crazy rock before God's altar.

Brute Fact

We love a face, a body
not for perfection of feature
or color or line, but simply
because they vanish.

All touching is transient.
The hand and what it holds dissolves.
For the open sore of loss
there is no unguent.

The most casual brush
of flesh lies heavy, and the spur
goading the lustiest loving
is not desire, but death.

Demon Child

All spring you would tease us,
dangling pale legs from the branches,
smirking at us through the leaves.

When the days turned to summer,
you woke damp and docile while
wind combed back your blond hair.

Then, heat's hissing snake
clenched in both fists, you pounce, shrieking
down horned and hoofed with the sun.

Exorcism

Father, glum ghost of Christmas Past,
if you are anywhere around,
I hope you are propitiated,
old Christmas-hater!

See here I make a holocaust
of all my childish Christmas loves:
My tears at Silent Night smoke upward,
orgasmic shivers

along the spine at Midnight Mass,
my dreams of cosy family fun
(smell the sweet savor of their stink),
my awe inside the stable

holding its nose at cow dung, really.
Rest, rest, ghost, childhood's god, and smile
now that I shrink from blasphemies,
those shams of love.

"Why Seems It So Particular with Thee?"

MEDITATION ON AN OLD CLICHE

Somebody's straight to somebody's crooked,
Somebody's gay to somebody's sad,
Somebody's good to somebody's wicked—
So said the girl whom nobody'd had.

Somebody's limber to somebody's crippled,
Somebody's last to somebody's first,
Somebody's sober to somebody's tippled—
So said the dry who's recovered the thirst.

Somebody's selfish to somebody's giving,
Somebody's soft to somebody's hard,
Somebody's dying to somebody's living—
So preached the fool to the terminal ward.

Somebody's pine to somebody's bush,
Somebody's work to somebody's fun,
And on Palestine hills the crosses bloomed lush,
Yet Christ saved the world on a particular one.

Open Question

"The intolerable concern for their health"—Thomas Merton

Do their kidneys fail or stroke
trip their wizened legs? By God,
nature plays some funny joke
on its children, for how odd
(since death wins by storm or stealth)
this intolerable concern for their health!

Do they die from being thin?
Do they die from being fat?
Never mind. Their common sin
is their marching onward flat-
footedly to waste their wealth
on intolerable concern for their health.

Do they die of cancer sneaking
through their cells? Or from the treason
riddling their own hearts? While reeking
of it, mortals pour as season,
preservative from mortal filth,
their intolerable concern for their health.

Brother, did you climb among
your companions rage by rage,
fear by fear and rung by rung,
then kick that ladder clear past age
and its petty commonwealth
of intolerable concern for their health?

Portrait of a Lady Playing Tit for Tat

You, growing weary of her mournful traps
Set for the wary prey of your affection
Have learned to foil them with a slight deflection
Easier than running miles, a little lapse
More practical than murder, love's catnaps
Affording you at least as much protection
From her as hibernations could. Perhaps.

But do you note a tinge of difference
In her, a crying fainter than before,
The echo, even, of your frantic mood?
For now she stalks an atmosphere less dense,
A cooler clime, that she may more and more
Wear its light arrogance of solitude.

After a Recital of Emily Dickinson
Set to Music

FOR M. F.

We stammer at love
Enunciate our rage
As knives or bullets shave,
Precisely, yet begrudge

Our gentle words, and will,
As only true hearts can,
Prove unoriginal
That prime primeval sin.

Since, thus, if Paul speaks clear,
Creation's spark plugs miss—
By friendship one small star
May shiver back to place.

Shamefaced Prayer

God, let me know you, not knowing that I know,
As sleepers do when locked in such embrace
Of dream they think they have not dreamed, although
I wonder how I come to the bad grace
To make this prayer contorted in an anger
Drilled deep as my past is, old as I am,
Twisting in fear, fed by such hunger
To claw my pain it makes faith half a sham.
For I who have lain down with dogs of doubt
Get up with all their fleas of bitterness,
Rubbed raw with scratching them, and head to foot
With rash of maybe's, if's, and but's, prove less
Than saint, unless a saint is merely one
Who, knowing need, must know it to the bone.

In Quiet Neighborhoods

*O Lord, raise up, we pray thee, thy power, and come
among us, and with great might succour us, that whereas
through our sins and wickedness, we are sore let and hindered
in running the race that is set before us, thy bountiful grace and
mercy may speedily help and deliver us; through Jesus Christ
our Lord, to whom, with thee and the Holy Ghost, be honour
and Glory, world without end. Amen.*—The Collect for the 4th
Sunday in Advent

I

Now that watch fires are out, monsters tormented,
murdered, lassoed, confined to dull extinctions,
caught on our barbed wire kindness, the wild moon
Diana no longer, merely rock admired
by men who skim its surface, lumbering ghosts
found more miraculous than myth or fable—
no sheep may safely graze our savage lawns.

Now that our streets are washed of any spoor
fouler than poodle droppings, sidewalks swept
until they sparkle brighter than some heaven
the spirit rattling like a rotting pod
inside the precious body coached to die
in five neat steps to brain waves' subtle titter—
sleepers awake all night from dread of nothing.

Now that our ambulances strung with sirens
can outrace Pegasus to save our skulls
broken before their time, good angels hurried
to rescue us, all only good friends bound
toward death's dark cradle, swift as galaxies
upon whose runners night with us is flying.

II

Now that all truth is numbed till cold as coins
On Pilate's eyes, as numbed as the dry veins
knotted in Judas' neck, a handshake all

the cover any liar needs, a smile
the sole disguise for folly fools require
sneaking among their well-trimmed shrubs—how brightly
all night the morning star gains on their mischiefs.

Now that our homes are guarded from ourselves,
we being burglars picking our own locks
attempting to get home by any means
to places that were never meant for ours,
the heart of each of us a clock whose hands
have stopped forever at one hour, we sit
here weeping all night long the night away.

Now that amid our lives we drooped besotted,
riding our cars and airplanes minus hands,
or hear the whisper from our waters bathed in,
"Lie down, it is so warm," or, finally,
we plant our fields with dream distractions till
they crawl the whole world—we intone
all night, "Komm susser, Tod, dear sister, brother."

III

Now that God's eyes enclose no Christmas sleep,
Nor His Good Friday's spell (such gods have eyes
that shut and open, dolls a child delights in,
playthings of times and seasons, antiseptic churches
where poets and Christians caught on guard must fidget)—
our lights enrage the darkness mothering mild,
the rose of all desiring bloomed unnoticed.

Now that the darkness swells with grace and judgment,
menace and mercy wrestling on the wind
risen with leaves and rain like buoyant banners
stitched with the name higher than every name,
muffled hosannahs hailing true Son of God,
true Son of our shuddering flesh—He makes
our hearts all night seeded with light rejoice.

Now that our feast of lights forbids the famished
from our tight doors, none fastened in but us
who merely dream of being broken into
with every footfall only falling branches
or rutting cats creeping beneath the hedges
as dogs wake up to chase—come, Savior of
us, the ungentle, Holy Thief of night!

Against Daylight Saving Time

When I was a child
light wandered freely
over the sky,

in summer
sweetly dressing
early risers and late sleepers,

going out to get the paper, my father
a second sun
to my drowsy eyes

before I melted back to dark
curled in a shaving of dream
in a corner of morning.

Now light is snapped
back and forth across the country
on mechanical strings.

Fall

Light, whose limping whisper was thought,
snagged upon inertia,
knotting into lumps.

Light, whose last throes the eyes captured,
tangled in itself,
jumbling into clods.

Light, one time God's pseudonym,
ground from the guts of sun,
straining into turds of thing and stuff.

Light, descending from self-contemplation,
matted to matter, clotted to shape,
clabbering to arms and legs and faces.

Unalterable

Into the language of the dead
our words, translated, mean the same—
grief, anger, love, hate.
Still their lips utter the same words,
striking our ears with the same tones.
Vainly we listen for a different message.
From that far land of unfamiliar landmarks
forever we must hear the dead reciting
their old set pieces.

Eden Revisited

"We'll talk all night until we swoon away," you promised,
friend of my innocence and of no more than that,
the only rule allowing for such talk.

&

Words were my lawyers once before Judge Life.
Now when he passes sentence,
silence and I stand side by side.

No longer are words the currency of my country.
I have been thrown into jail
more times than one for passing counterfeit.

&

My mother's best friend gave a leaf to her.
She recorded it in words by writing,
"Given to me in 1912 by Helen."

Though Freud was lurking those days in Vienna,
people still spoke.

And those two girls, my mother and Helen,
not knowing that Victoria was dead,
moved inside their skins as though not touching them.

So now I view their leaf, more durable than breath,
but bruised and breaking under each minute more
frayed reconciliation between truth and lie.

Dining Room Eucharist

FOR MIKE CORRIGAN

With offhand elegance and unkempt grace,
Young whirlwind blowing from the Southern wild,
You said the Mass and watched my small dog chase,
Romping around your feet, and only smiled.
Unswayed by fripperies of priestly pomp,
You stood in your worn blue jeans, looking up
To where you saw no God but in the swamp
Of circumstance, and with the bread and cup
You blessed Him, mildly bowed before a Lord
You well know would not have His creatures cringing.
My clock chimed that same moment; if you heard
You gave no sign. Mere dignity impinging
Upon your strict attention would distract
From this resplendence of the naked act.

Worrying the World

I worry the world,
intractable bone
breaking my teeth
until it has shattered out of its shape
of dirt, daub, and dung,
grinding it down
finer than atoms
in the mills of my mind
crushed out of its matter
back to its chaos
dusting my palm
a fine mess of shadow.
By blowing its motes
the shape of my breath
I worry the world.

Study in White

FOR THE REVEREND HELEN M. HAVENS

A white benignity
moves at the altar,
an air of elegant holiness

whose source is the vein
apulse in the throat
threading blue against white,

whose roots tangle deeper
cleaving the soil
where, white downed with darkness,

all crisscrossed, I bow
beyond question and answer,
the white smoke of words

moving over my mouth,
white noise of the ego.
Mothering Silence,

here may the wafer
touched to my tongue
leave your white prayer in my mind.

The Inescapable Day

Lord! here it is again
and here we are too
neither we nor the Day up to par.

Some year, we swear, we'll avoid it,
turkey seasoned with squabbles making for indigestion,
too much wine a sure inoculation against much joy

as Murphy's Law pecks away even at Christmas.
Maybe it was so even from the first,
the shepherds with muddy boots trampling down Mary's sleep.

In fact, so hearsay has it, in the Primal Time
Lucifer plummeted to his age-long pique
because the Lord had pledged to become a bellowing baby.

Had He nothing better to do? demanded the eldest Angel.
Well, no, apparently not. So, here we fidget, snuffling and
    straining
to work the Mystery over our heads and hearts like a child's
    pajamas.

Post-Christmas Prayer

Lord, born in winter's draft
of dream, all seasons lie,
for time is of our making,

craftiness of our craft,
fine art of treachery;
therefore, go with us breaking

these gilded branches up,
tearing the tinsel down,
trampling the plastic star

lest their detritus stop
our lungs that choke upon
debris such trappings are.

Call us to step into
a chill lost in the finest
of painted snowscapes sold

as greetings, and with You go
where stripped boughs write honest
calligraphy of cold.

What Really Happens

We are the cat who worries time away,
tossing it hither, *thunk*, and thither, *thwack*,
tail twitching, while between its paws its prey
flops back and forth and back
until the feline master of the house,
with time, poor thing routinely mauled to sweeten
monotony, forgets that time's the mouse
that kills in being eaten.

Prudent

I dip a cautious foot in the Atlantic
Of generosity, yet keep my wits
To draw it out in time before I panic.
I give myself away by modest bits
In crumbs fed birds of dainty appetite.
I give my love out in judicious doles.
Mine is the wise man's, not the widow's mite,
Leaving in my largesse enough loopholes
Through which I may escape if necessary
To practicality. For, though no miser,
Conservative and not reactionary—
I shun those few whose goodness is a geyser,
Who cannot comprehend a balance sheet
And fling their lives like pennies at God's feet.

Awkward Good-byes

I am sorry I seldom speak   I
am losing my knack   I
remember the language but poorly.

Though God knows I used it well, spoke it
better than you even   I
take small pride in such talent   I

sucked it up more easily than mother's
milk. It must taste sweeter
to odd palates. Anyhow I'm

craving amnesia, the happy kind,
since whatever pig-
latin we talked, none called it love.

After Reading of Helen Keller

Mind, unworthy of tragedies that befall us,
holds up to the hurricane its twelve inch ruler
snapped immediately and borne away.

Love, now, none of your pale-eyed professors,
who have their uses, but not here
when the patient would die while they debate,

jumps over the puddle of questions and answers,
gets straight to its work wrenching the cross
the odd shapes of salvation.

Pigself

Pigself seeks to be delicate
swaying to spirit's music,
but trips up its own feet.

Pigself, a poor drunkard and glutton
for visions, roots among them
and backs off with a blush.

Still, pigself needs to remember
how its lush poverty
provides its alphabet

of grunts, groans, snuffles, and snorts
so that spirit can spell
even the word for God.

Reassurance

When you shake hands with my pains,
you know each crease of their palms,
the angle at which they hold
a teacup, read their slightest
tremor precisely for what
it is, follow them upstairs
and lie down among them, less
like Daniel among lions
than a mother with children.
Worry is only a glove
you've tried on and thrown away.
We won't need it any more.

Christopher,

you bear a good name
given in no baptism
but that of your mother's waters,

named for the brawny saint
who bore Christ over a surly river,
child grown heavier than a coffin,

weighed with the weight once borne for you;
so bear Him, who bares the truth's
lightning against the nights:

This wish I wish you in whispers,
this gift I give you in secret,
not mine to will true or give you

and only yours in the reaching
that dear and difficult span
of all your years.

Christmas in Dark Times

Christmas still comes in spite of death and taxes.
Or, rather, because of them, else why should God
Have become human? Surely when Heaven annexes
Itself to earth, this feat can be no odd
Whim of indulgence. All our careless moments
Spring up like green grass, all our loves and laughter
Burst forth like leaves and flowers in mild climates.
Our play, our feasts, our sex require a softer
Touch than the terrible assault of grace.
At natural births an angel's an upstart.
The crib and cross of Christ are out of place,
Rocking the balance of the summer heart.
No blithe vacationer, God comes anew,
Seeing that death is what we have to do.

Light Poem

FOR ALL OF US

Let's talk, good friend, with minds bareassed and sober,
Hiding behind no barriers but ourselves
Which are no barriers. It's late, at least October;
With years behind tucked on their lonesome shelves.
It'll be tough, yet such an effort's valiant
At any rate; and then, we'll have it done.
And we shall have long ages to lie silent.
Oh yes, all right, there's Heaven, but earth's fun,
For all its crap, shit, fuck you too, unholy,
This trinity, and yet not wholly bad.
So leave us talk, slowly, still not too slowly,
Considering what time's already had
Drinking us down—and now with dreadful thirst
When it's (who knows) December thirty-first?

Liebestod

If I could merge myself into the country
Of trees and shrubs and where the air flows pure
Over my head, so battered by the sentry
Of fixed identity, to find a cure
In being neither beast nor man nor woman
Nor even poet, nor, sweet Jesus! cripple,
I might be something else, both rare and common
Combing the grasses of the coastal plain
We traveled Sunday easy as a smile,
And think I might at last shake off my pain,
But steel-gilt buildings, hidden less each mile,
Sprout blooming pallid hues of the horizon,
Tall toadstools delicate with dawn—and poison.

Love's Bitten Tongue

FOR CHRISTOPHER, MY LAST NEPHEW, IN HOPE

1

Lord, hush this ego as one stops a bell
Clanging, cupping it softly in the palm.
Should it make music, silence it as well,
For there's no difference when one wants calm
Of silence from the ego's loud tinnitus
Buzzing in spirit's ear with no relief,
With every reverence a false hiatus
Which brings those moments I name prayer to grief,
Tempts me to think I better honor them
By turning away from prayer as I did once.
So my thoughts, snared by their own strategem,
Like balls that children toss aside, all bounce
In my head back and forth until despair
Of praying may, in mercy, become prayer.

2

Of praying may (in mercy become prayer)
My backward journey be—Christ, teach me this!
This trek begun and left when, hope to spare
I saw ahead a new metropolis
All burnished brightly with an innocence
Now peeled the same as paint from ancient houses,
Its steel now buckled like a picket fence,
And found, that built for worship or carouses,
Buildings will suffer tediums of age,
As buildings must, as mine must too too soon.
So, may I never mind if I engage
The winks and titters from the ones who've known
Me from my wanderer's days and wisely nod
As His old daughter toddles home to God.

3

As His old daughter toddles home to God,
She sees she might have shunned her detour, bloody

276

With self all cut upon itself, the road
Looking so spacious, but rocky, rutted, muddy,
In fact, she can recall a wiser woman
Who all her life has walked with faithful calm
With angels, demons, and the merely human,
Each balanced like a baby on her palm.
And now that she has settled into years
More lightly than a ballerina sinks
Into her split, so having worn out tears
And laughter too, this wise old woman drinks
Her morning coffee as if sculpted, rare
Reality, Praise Seated in a Chair.

4

Reality, praise seated in a chair,
Is sweet as any lauds a church may utter,
And my typewriter ticks a better prayer
Than does, except by chance, my pious stutter
Half faking faith and hope and, God knows, love
As if I should invite a friend to talk
About some enterprise, but should remove
My thoughts allowing them to take a walk.
Whereas my poem must, being a true-
Born of my sweat, aim straight and hit its center,
My bastard prayer that I less birth than hew
Out of my wooden block of self must splinter
Every direction—pain, terror, grief, and feuding—
All four horizons of my hunger, brooding.

5

All four horizons of my hunger brooding,
Like giant's fingers they have closed upon me,
Leaving their prints upon my throat, intruding
Upon my lucky limbo here, they spawn me,
Their doubles, literal, imaginary
And terrify me till I cannot stir,
Dog hunkered under thunder-claps and wary
Of foes she cannot see or touch, her fur

Beruffled by the harsh strokes of her shiver.
I wonder, preyed upon by self-derision,
Daimon, demon, myself, who is that dumb contriver
Of shadow, substance, vapor's stuff and vision?
Still Lord, I hunt that name, that name I can
But hunt again, again, and yet again.

6

But hunt again, again, and yet again—
"Lord Jesus Christ, have mercy upon me!" Strange
Hunting halloo, yet stranger prey that can
Hunt down the hunter on this narrow range
Ribbing those depths beyond repose, past eddy
In any cramping blind that keeps me coward
Who'd stalk the weak and hide my puny body.
From fear of my own death—or, turning seaward
For sport, I change my weapon, take a net,
Like Peter tired out with his toil of sorrow
Returned to rest his heart in the stale sweat
His fathers eased theirs in from hurt and harrow
Find his same Lord refreshed to more than match me
Crying, "Great Fish, once netted unnamed, catch me!"

7

Crying "Great Fish, once netted unnamed, catch me!
Turn fisherman and net me Yours by magic
Of nature, grace, water, or word to snatch me
Out of my death," I so confess love's logic
None of my own can probe, Jesus, but never
Mind niceties of such names—save me drowning
Deep in the muck of myself, shallow river
Stagnating of myself and always running
More like a poem struggling toward its aim
More like dream flashes morning minds resist.
From what I am not make me what I am,
Nothing compared to You, Your towelled waist
Ever before me as once You walked the round
Frail earth small as my heart made holy ground.

8

Frail earth small as my heart made holy ground,
Small as all other hearts You render holy,
We tread on one another's soil and grind
Under our feet the human grace that slowly
Is worn away, forgetting in our rush
To put our shoes aside and stand in awe
Of friends and strangers, every one the bush
Burning with You, my God—whom Moses saw
And did not see, Dark Brightness, much too dark
Beating His eyeballs with the desert sun,
Whom Paul ran headlong into with no mark
Of sense, Bright Darkness, how You might be One
Of us, another poor son of a sea
Creature flung to the shore of mortal eye.

9

Creature flung to the shore of mortal eye,
A stranger to Your mother thirty years
After her rapture of angels gave way
To neighbors' titters and their outraged jeers,
Stranger to Yourself, forever an orphan,
Calling God Father because You were lonely,
Riding the heave of my planet, sea-urchin,
The sound of Your splash echoed thinly
As mine among the galaxies clustered
Uncanny coral reefs smothering thought
And peeled down at last to a body blistered,
Bared to be needled by sun and turned out
To the hurt of the how, You, God soured acrid
Sweat, my poor Brother, so locked up Your secret.

10

Sweat, my poor Brother, so locked up Your secret
Its key by death will have been thrown away.
Nobody's concern, profa one or sacred,
Any more, any less than mine shall be;
History's Hobby that some pedant's shears

279

Shapes to a whim, Your life the same stuff
Of time as mine, the same days and years,
Hanged for a felon on *maybe* and *if*—
Think on Your groans no one heard but Your Father,
Your last thought, Your last sigh breathed on the Cross—
No hand plucks them and no fingers can gather
These snowflakes melting so swiftly they dress
The air this moment their wanness has stung
You, my God, lonesome man, Love's bitten tongue.

11

You, my God, lonesome man, Love's bitten tongue,
Heaven's incredible wound, You who made
This world split in half, Your birth bade me hang
As a Texas child on edge in my bed
All Christmas Eve between waking and sleeping
Waiting to find out what mystery broke
In sounds more melodious than sleighbells sweeping
Over my roof or than huge bangs that woke
Sweet silent night as I wondered each boom
If I could go see what Santa Claus left;
So, caked with the mud of myself, I still dream
Hollow and holy and merrily cleft
Between fireworks' flash and the narrow space
For Your cradle, between greed and Your grace.

12

For Your cradle between greed and Your grace
Shadows Your Cross, which grown to pain's size
And sin's shape have required, Your love's device
For my love's lacking, my lapse of praise
For the life You have given, for my languor
Deep as the caverns of bellies so swollen
With emptiness that they half forget hunger;
I gnaw the bone of ingratitude, suddenly crave
To taste what cannot be tasted, my God,
To drink what I cannot drink, what You give
Through Your time to mine, as sustenance, food,

Angels' and children's, Your love's oblation—
The melting parable of incarnation.

13

The melting parable of incarnation
Has tabernacled on my tongue most simple,
Doubled no doubt by doubt, condition
Unfit to wit of Your ways, clumsy temple,
Sheltering never Your words but Your silence
Housing my mind to be housed in my heart,
Or rather housing heart and mind in balance.
Terrible two locked in terrible sport,
Under Your fierce sun should dry up the pond
Of my eyesight, should burn up, should wither
In those wastes of Your splendor gone beyond
All those comfortable words that would gather
My beloved Stranger, My strange Beloved,
To my mouth, O, that O, where my words orbit.

14

To my mouth, O, that O, where my words orbit,
To my mind that would play out, if it could,
Their meaning, to my heart that need not probe it
To the hot root of me finding it good—
You have come surely, a parent who aches
For the children's least cry rousing the tiger
That, striped with shadows of pain and fear, strikes,
Padded with whispers, but hungry and eager
With fact and sullen with dream, both together,
The Seem being Is and Is being Seem,
I call upon You, my Own and my Other—
Touch and lift me from reality's dream,
White snow light on my tongue, flake melting airy
That which broke, so they tell, as sunlight through Mary.

15

That which broke, so they tell, as sunlight through Mary
Was, Joseph felt, since first he held trembling

Close to himself her girlhood but a flurry
Of leaves in autumn whose last days fall tumbling
Upon steel air and against iron wind
Of winter nights which must come wherever
My homeland may be; so Jesus, remind
Me again and again how no life can cover
Its long end long and how no time is right
As You found out also when You have come straying,
Ignorant Baby newborn Christmas night,
Making me face beyond every gainsaying,
Past faith, past fear of that least, most dread foe,
Your birth is Love's Yes, Your death is Love's No.

16

Your birth is Love's Yes, Your death is Love's No
As Your Yes is Love's birth, Your No Love's death,
Your Way the End as Your End is the Way
Beyond courage and cowing, faith unfaith.
Therefore teach me, and I shall have been learned
And so learned that I shall have been taught,
But with an alphabet that has been burned
Into my bones, a book till now shut
And You unseal it, O Lamb only worthy
To read its alphabet scattered until
I offer it up, steel filings to smithy
Beaten out on the anvil, syllable
After slow syllable, You bid me dumb
Past hubbub hushing, sleep waking, steal home.

17

Past hubbub hushing, sleep waking, steal home
From the ways of the world into the wilds
Of Your ways, oh my Lord and give me the time,
Thief in the night, and save me from the folds
Of their lies, spare me the lures of their fancy
Deliver me from the traps of their tongues
Licking the spit of their lips raw and raunchy
Deliver me to the freedom to hang

Onto Your hem and walk the waves of terror
When the world treads down the fable of fact
To see but its own false face in the mirror
To reveal how its libels all conflict—
Go with me now to the time when I die.
Go with me God, You of the single eye!

18

Go with me God, You of the single eye
Boring a hole through the double-fanged dealers
Caught in the middle of their crooked way,
Though the nimble-footed and as loose-lipped as sailors
Or as I am, my Lord, when I lie down
To the doom of my dumbness when it wakes
And do not get up all pretty to plan
And will not bow down to somebody's balking.
Go with me, God, of the furrowed face
Set toward Jerusalem and none turns back
Though You must ride in on the back of an ass
And knowing full well what end You must make
With Your eyes on the ground to keep You humble',
Most High One, seeing how donkeys can stumble.

19

Most High One, seeing how donkeys can stumble
You pass calmly by to cast out the traders
Eager to trade with God through the shudders
Of their sheep and oxen, poor beasts that scramble
Under the flail of Your eyes sharp with love
Only the flail of Your hair loosed with justice,
Then calmly and gently and patiently move
From Your passion's discourse to its practice,
To a friend's chamber and under the trees
Where Your prayers groaning with labor
While John whinnies, James snores, and Peter brays
How loyalty has his heart for a harbor
Till at last You hang bound, most agile of runners
More terrible than an army with banners.

20

More terrible than an army with banners,
Your body spread on the cross for fine linen,
Its beauty a banquet for this sorry sinner's
Prime predilection, made Magdalene's paean
Paid for Your fairness, Your slender neck, chalice
Your navel, paten, Yourself wine and bread
In Your Father's hands, meek God without malice
As meek as the Dove who still broods overhead
As She did long ago over dark waters
Of Creation, above the flood of Noah
And brought forth anew an earth of sweet odors
When stars of morning sang out alleluia
Under Your feet and around Your entrancing
Their pulses with joy, mine also dancing.

21

Their pulses with joy, mine also dancing,
Your angels will sing me songs through the night
When the terrors of death and Hell seem enticing
My heart to fly to the hovels that wait
My flesh to huddle, a fetus of fear,
In some circle of love imagined sweet,
Keener from fancy than chilly spring air
Of a gray Easter day whose dawn will greet
Your resurrection not seen by one eye
When You shake off Your shrouds, no longer covered,
Mercury morning star striking gaze,
Diamond bedded against Burgundy velvet
Till Magdalene comes dew-sodden and weary
Being pierced open by Your whisper, "Mary."

22

Being pierced open by Your whisper, "Mary . . ."
The woman gapes at Your gardener's clothes
Messy with muck and juices of bud and berry,
Offence to eye, delectation to nose.
So You have opened me to woe and wonder

Much sharper than woe, far keener than pain
Pitching the techniques of thought that might pander
To the gimmicks of mind, but split open mine
That prays, "What shall I do, Jesus? How deal
With those flesh-splitting throbs, pain, dread, rapture
Which rupture my being drooping and dull
To the literal Word, ecstatic scripture?
How may I do it, Great Alpha, Omega
Unless I bow, acolyte to my ego."

The
Sun
Has
No
History
1981

Subterfuge

I remember my father, slight,
staggering in with his Underwood,
bearing it in his arms like an awkward bouquet

for his spastic child who sits down
on the floor, one knee on the frame
of the typewriter, and holding her left wrist

with her right hand, in that precision known
to the crippled, pecks at the keys
with a sparrow's preoccupation.

Falling by chance on rhyme, novel and curious bubble
blown with a magic pipe, she tries them over and over,
spellbound by life's clashing in accord or against itself,

pretending pretense and playing at playing,
she does her childhood backward as children do,
her fun a delaying action against what she knows.

My father must lose her, his runaway on her treadmill,
will lose the terrible favor that life has done him
as she toils at tomorrow, tensed at her makeshift toy.

Lullaby for My Mother

Now I would sing you at last
a lullaby you never sang me,
a lullaby no mother could sing:

When you are dying
now while the days are so lovely
I feel I could take them into my body.

Here, then, take them into your body
inhale the blue sky, drink the sun
through the tall crystal of air

while cicadas chime their long sanctus
low in your ear—all is yours
as it never could be until now.

Dark Mother

My mother, you, when well, forgot me, your first-born
you never bore, whom no man got upon you save a dream
more childish than your youngest: you desired a doll,
cunning, if broken. But when it moved
and howled and kicked and spat, you threw it down
with disappointment and disgust. It's too late.
I'm nearly as old as you are. Nobody can
mother us, either one, save that black mother,
kindly, if cruel, whose arms reach for us all
drawing us down and down and back and back
into her winding sheets of womb. Nobody likes her summons
late in the evening. She sings her lullaby
through a mouth cracking and cackling from long calling.

Reluctant Confession

One time I wondered what somebody meant when he wrote me,
"The sky seems closer somehow when we lose our mothers."
Now I know you are dead I am afraid of the stars.

I had always feared them, but I saw them through your fingers,
though you could do nothing about deep space, its black holes
pulsating stealthily to gobble up everything.

And though I did not need you, I said, nor even
want you, I thought, yet you loomed near in remoteness
like absent God, mother and God turned true by cliché.

Dear Non-Necessity, speak with some irritation.
Tell me to wink my eye and see the heavens pushed back
not needing the weight of your weak and restraining palms.

On Finding an Old Snapshot

Squinting into a lost sun,
you stand with me in the foreground,
knobby-kneed, spastic, shadow
of the world's groping fingers

from which you kept edging away,
eluding mind's intimate touch,
cold to the crude kiss of fact,
ascetic forced to get drunk,

passing through your existence
always obliquely, bleeding
a little at every corner
of definition, each name

by which you were called, an alias
poorly learned and remembered,
wearing your life like clothes
intended for somebody else.

Now with your child's suitcase of secrets
packed full, you have run off
into the dark I saw waiting
back of your elsewhere eyes.

Wild Child

We shoo death away,
tracking through our minds
with his muddy footprints—

waif, wild child snubbed,
kin unacknowledged,
shunted into shadow,

small enough to hide
on the outskirts of each breath,
holding no grudge,

peering from between his fingers
through which he will sift us, warming
their wanness upon our dust.

My body and her pleasure
no longer clap each other on the back
or fall into each other's arms,

but greet warily
as two old friends
who have grown fragile,

or maybe even hostile,
each carrying a razor
in her purse,

the death seed stirring
in flesh folds since birth
to dawdle along my tall and narrow bones.

Incantation with a Camera

Even bad photos have their own life:
The dog, turned old, sitting by the steps,
the girl, now dead, making a face in the driveway,
her clowning long turned solemn.

Come in, come in, they whisper,
these countenances, into our world
your memory skews right
beyond the makeshift magic of technology,

and dance with us standing still,
stand still in dancing.
Hold to us through our leave-taking,
yet leave us holding, holding . . .

Summation

I move among you and
you turn from me like
leaves of a sensitive
plant, but now it scarcely
rates a yawn, loneliness
being the dew that melts
in solitude's sun,
since I have discovered
the court of my childhood
burned down, the halls of its
approval collapsed, and
have come home to myself
here in my homemade world.

View from a Small Garden

Buildings rise tall, temporary,
buckle of air, warping of light,
speck on the iris, sight's happy flaw:
cars skim, mote after mote:
mechanics made artifice of summer,
centered into itself, a wind,
invisible centipede, testing my face,
cicadas mowing thick grass of silence.

Southern Colonial

You with the spread wings of your wide porches,
walking your floors must be like flying,
billowing full of sun and wind;

your halls are surely burnished bright with laughter,
your stairways brought to a high sheen with tears,
your brass antiqued by time's amber luster.

Two souls should live in you who must be married
less in each other than in life
as birds seem rooted in the air,

in you that clothe instead of house them,
breathed from the richness of their beings
as the exhalation of earned grace.

Bike Ride

FOR PAT IN PASSING

We could not get along,
so when I wheel along
the street you stumbled down
where as the light leaps down
along these Sunday ways
as sleepers keep the ways
of night after night fades—
your ghost pales, but not quite fades.

Sadly I shrug it by,
continuing rolling by
the bungalows and lawns,
the papers on the lawns
stirless as snoozing pets.
Sharper than newsprint pets,
a dog that my scent wakens
staggers up and barks and wakens.

Old times I next ride into
here where high walls sweep into
mansions foursquare as visions
not for your pennies, visions
men hammered in brick and wood,
this rosy brick, white wood
as real as my flesh, as lively,
where the affluent dead sleep lively.

Now, turning home, I pass
over new routes to pass
where some girl, thin as a flute,
plays her sweet godless flute
and glimpse the morning moon,
blanched, bitten host, this moon
left over from darkness, holds.
Like your ghost, paled. Yet it holds.

Time and Mary Jean

You are where you are.
Every moment consumes you.
Our major concerns—

cars in no-park zones,
buns in the oven, damp laundry
unironed and mildewing—

you take off like armor
worn by warier folk who dress
in the past and the future.

For wholly content
with the merest minute, you
go naked in now.

Stepped from your last second,
you will bequeath us a statue
of time in your shape.

After Guyana

Evil moves in a straight line.
Evil is simple.
Evil gets from here to there.

Evil speaks small words.
Evil counts, One, two, three.
Evil piles brick on brick on brick.

Evil knows its mind.
Evil never says, "But on the other hand . . ."
Evil is tidy.

Evil has no parts to break.
Evil, being death's other face.
Evil is pure, is single.

Public Address

The great man splinters
out of his block of wood
scaring children who thought he never moved.

His smile creaks by
on pulleys, and his grace
is only by the grace of block and tackle.

Some day we'll take him
into our grief, death snowing
his angles down into a corpse.

Senility

Old mind, nosing toward death,
broken turtle half out of its shell,
poking around in the thinning air,
can't you squirm back again,
you! flopping along with your shell still intact.

No, your final curiousness
has got you in trouble,
snooping among the Last Things,
has taken you far too far,
wriggling along, stupid joke,
too slow with the punch line.

Exile

Wrenched from the wiles of your truth,
lost on the lawns of our fiction
somewhere between birdsong and Bach—

you walk the wavering ways of our affection,
bleeding sometimes from our pavements,
your tongue lolling in a put-on laugh,

your secret unparsed by our grammars,
tell me: who can be silent enough
to speak with you?

Strangers

Animals fix us with their gaze,
yet we are no more than islands
in the oceans of their vision.

In stares of dog and cat no less
than hawk and cobra our atolls
lie. So Jesus is called Lamb.

For in their liquid glances God
and His dumb creatures, innocent,
wash the frail reef of the human.

The Sun Has No History

The sun has no history,
the leaves keep no diary,
that bird on that limb feels no nostalgia,
nor did the water remember the slosh of our feet,
my sister's and mine, in the worn wash tub,
nor did the hot wax of air take the imprint
of my aunt's chuckling voice,
"Land sakes! You all sing it like a dirge,"
Revive Us Again, which she had heard lively.
No, because days are sculptured from space,
shaped out of sizzling motes,
hammered from heat-waves.

Seasons repeat themselves,
babble syllables innocent of order.
Hours leave no fingerprints
for sleuths of memory to trace.
Last year camouflages itself
under the light of this instant
slanting upon me who comb
the green of this bush,
the red of that bloom,
the stuff of clouds overhead here
turning to me forever
familiar faces of strangers.

The sun has no history.
Only I, bearing
my Adam and Eve on my back,
dragged under, dragged down, may leap
up to the saddle of hope.

Naming What We Love

FOR COVENANT BAPTIST CHURCH

We'll form a committee to discuss the Second Coming
and talk our way out of the Last Judgment,
not to mention holding debates with death
as to the appropriate time for its arrival—

Because, had we only known the way to say it,
our world and hence our lives would have turned out better.
It is strange, you know, what hangs on the turn of a phrase.
For instance, the connective *and* once split the Church like an
    apple.

Galileo hauled in his drowning integrity on the reel, "But it
    does,"
and under the Nazi noose Bonhoeffer spun out his threads so
    precious
we have inched across them with a tremulous tread
uncertain whether we'd fall through them and to which Abyss.

Therefore, dear friends, it is no joking matter—
straining in deadpan tones to name what we name so badly
that nobody could guess we might love what we wanted—
with our tongues bitten raw, pinched between mum and
    mumbling.

When the Living Is Easy

Today the poem is outside me where somehow it should be,
not within me like my own tooth I am trying to pull.
It is more like a child tugging me out of my sleep,
more like a fish on a hook when the fishing is fine.

For sure, the thing's not a tiger to stalk down my peace,
still less a hidden disease that feeds me feeding it,
or some craziness strutting about in musical uniform,
nor even Solomon's wine that stings like an adder.

No, lounging at home in my habit hugged by its warmness,
blasphemous, nearly, at ease, yawning my words to bed,
I say, "Come back in the morning."
Was this Bach's serene excitement (a little),
how he moved, riding the random airs to their stable of glory . . .

Emily Dickinson Comes to the Dinner Party

We could have done better by you
whose lover we never tracked down
a woman
a man
or at your tether's end God maybe
kept guessing
at you who were virginal
in the sense that discounts any other
never reckoning you
giving no readings
conducting no workshops
and how many poems did you publish two three?
touching people
needed only to sing
single
singular
touching yourself
so
dare we
serve you up on a platter
simpering
Eat me.

Dramatic Monologue in the Speaker's Own Voice

I walk naked under my clothes like anyone else,
and I'm not a bomb to explode in your hands.
Of course, you are not (I would not accuse you of)
thinking of holding me down, but of holding me up.
Yet sometimes I'd love to be eased from the envelope of sleep,
stroked gently open (although it would take some doing—
on my part, that is). My lost virginity
would hurt me the way the ghosts of their limbs
make amputees shriek, my womanhood
too seldom used. Have you ever viewed me this way?
No, none of you ever have. I'm either a monster
in search of a horror movie to be in,
or else I'm a brain floating within a body
whose sides I must gingerly touch while you glance
discreetly away. Sometimes when you hear it go—bump!
it gives you a nasty shock after which you insist I am glued
to my flesh like a fly in a paste pot. Maybe you think
     everyone is,
that, or a delicate lady in a dirty sty mincing on tiptoe.
I wish you'd learn better before we all totter
into our coffins where there's no straight way to lie crooked.

As Usual

My books, my sulky joys, lie here neglected
while I go perilously armed with poetry,
a weapon I grow careless with like some fool boy
who clambers over a fence and shoots himself in the foot.

He'd be better off at home and so might I.
Still I needn't worry when soon enough
I shall be clinging to a book with bloody fingernails,
repelling the dark face of myself,
using each fraying word for foothold, ropes creaking and
      straining,
spy back from a failed mission, this time disguised
as some impatient patient, who fidgets and glances up
now and again while reading in death's anteroom.

An Essay in Criticism by Way of Rebuttal

Every white page is
the threat of infinite snow.

Every descent into silence is
the risk of never returning.

Every tentative word is
in peril of being wanting.

Every poet knows
what the saint knows

that every new day is
to retake the frontier of one's name.

Another Sleep Poem

Sleep seduces me
better than the lovers that I never had
ever could.

Sleep can comfort me
better than shabby prayers I always say
never do.

Sleep can console me
better than alcohol that rakes my guts
ever will.

But, friends, best of all,
far more than death sleep soothes me,
when, during the night, we wake to kiss each other—

Death has no mouth.

Prayer to My Muse

The door is closing

where ghosts hide,
where gods hide,
where even I hide.

I'm none too sorry,
longing to be back
coiled in my wombworld,

too smug and small, I know,
no wider than my bed
where no one sleeps but me.

Still, crack the door a little,
stepmother muse to show
a night light burning.

If I
Had
Wheels
Or
Love

UNCOLLECTED

POEMS

Thanksgiving: Theme and Variations

Lovely lady, dressed in white,
how can I requite you,
filling every day and night
with God's Son to light you,
flooding every night and day
with white witchery
leading me along the way
you would follow, free,
elegant, your easy grace,
how be thanking you
giving me at least a place
standing tall and true!

Lovely lady, glowing white,
stand sterner, lest you falter.
Preaching Christ, you too must fight
always at His altar;
for you alter, bright to dark,
scaring me who love you
although I who take your spark
silver rapier, prove you
caring, even caring much
when I dare defy you
craving only your light touch
that mercy may not try you.

Lovely lady, sporting white,
wry, but rarely wicked,
what brave wonder, bold delight,
might you bear of crooked
I embraced with my whole self
yourself wholly, brush
the shadows of your throat, engulf
half your snowy hush,
hold, while slipping down to down,
all bitter and all sweet,

flowing swiftly, dusk till dawn,
to your dusty feet.

Lovely lady, priest in white,
mind these words which share
dreams and counsels old as light
on your cloudy hair,
old as fear to die alone,
whatever death may be,
lithe as life or stunned to stone,
pray, remain with me,
or else, should a distance take you
fast and firm of faith,
may someone remotely like you,
ease me onto death.

Hats

Sometimes I wear a cripple's hat and limp
A little sometimes a poet's hat and write a lot.
Sometimes I take a dream for a fiddle.
Sometimes I query the cosmos, grave child.
Sometimes if it would answer, I'd just shrug,
Tell it, tell all my friends, "Who cares?" Good-bye,
See you around. Sometimes I ease my bunions
And sneeze the beans clean out of my nose.
Sometimes I pray, now and then relish a chant.
Sometimes I'm like my old daddy, who swore,
"Those goddamned preachers don't know a damn!"
Sometimes I'd wear no hat, in fact, would go
Naked, nameless and numb, abreathing stone.

Love Song

You, smiling friend, say only that you like me,
And that, at least for now, is quite enough,
For I have had my fill with talk of love
Which mostly wears a grin, teeth bared to strike me,
Which reaches out its hands with nails to spike me,
Which hurries toward me on feet shod with rough
Boots all too set to kick me down and shove
Me in the mud and bleeding lift and hike me
Out to the dump where trusting fools belong
To get the just deserts that hopeful spirits merit
Then mock at them for rising bruised and sore
And go, "Tch, tch," when they don't sing a song.
And so, since one who says "I love"'s a ferret,
Just say, "I like you"—don't say any more!

A Word to the Wise

I'm moving forward, yet my past crowds in,
Racing ahead almost, passing me by,
If such were possible. The air grows thin
Because this ghost gang sucks the oxygen
Out of my lungs until I gasp and cry,
"Get out of my way for God's sakes!" How high
Their plaintive voices instantly reply,
"We cannot. We are you." Your own skin
Is not so close, for that is what you slough
Every few years till the end of your days,
While we both more and less than mist, allow
No one to lose us or to shake us off.
Hamlet and you remember—since always
Your human heart's clock hands stand still at *now*.

Holy Week

The churches grow hysterical with grief, and we
Who rarely shed a tear save for ourselves,
Wring corporate hands as the whole week dissolves
In the fogs and vapors of our misery
Over Your ancient pain we dare not see
Daily renewed as all the year revolves
On its axis of hurt and hate and crisscrossed loves
The air gone gummy with piousity—
We interrupt our fasts with artichoke
And cheese. (A few poor beasts exult
Maybe at being spared our gluttonous rages.)
Were such the reasons, Jesus, Your heart broke
And so broke from Your cross itself that bolt
Of furious charity upon the ages?

Spring Singsong

Mmmm growls the lawnmower,
its mechanized heart turned animal with spring and
silky with leaves
and
sharp whistles my man mowing as squirrel cocks its
ear
and *whop, whap* go those tall young guys
roofing the house next door and clumsy in all the
right places,
graceful in all the wrong
and
swish go the velvety ladies
yes, ah, yesyesyessing off by
and
my younger self's lost, lost
and hunches down in between yesterday's buildings
all hunkering down
among slenderest flowers of steel.

The Jolly Green Giant

I'm gone not a week, but already
my house has the smell of absence,
odor of emptiness.

The day leans light on the window,
an animal taking its time,
and yawning before it pounces.

The yard lies meekly prone,
a giant sleeping
and in no hurry.

He suffers his hair to be clipped
week by week, knowing
it will loop my home in its coils.

For Stringless Love

If I fall down even as those more lithe
Must do, for God's sake, hush your lamentation
For joy that then I'll rest on solid earth
And not on quicksands of imagination.
Yes, if my image buckles, blurs its structure,
Don't cry too long (and who knows, you might cry
Since everyone adores a pretty picture,
Yet pretty pictures wear the wary eye).
And, Hell, you're born too old for idols, dolls.
In fact, you've scarcely time for growing up
Before death hauls you down to her and lulls
You sound asleep upon her rumpled lap.
So, if I trip, take heart—you'll see me clear,
Polished upon my each particular.

Isn't This a Dainty Dish?

I, having found myself, have found my breast;
Viewed with the cache the dragon guarding it,
Not to be foiled by courage, prayer, or wit,
Nor told how to by savant or by priest.
The table's laid with my poor bones as feast.
Though I'm the guest of honor, bit by bit
I am not served but served up as I sit
Ripping the demon's gullet. Yet at least
Finality will have the elegance
Of being known beforehand and thus human
If not humane (surely a thing to praise).
My death bows low to me, signing my dance-
Card with his name, a gracious demon,
A gentleman bred in more courteous days.

By Way of Explanation

You need not thank me if I kiss your hand
As though I hailed some miracle moved image
Of piety that should be decked in plumage
Of pageantry, of virtue on demand.
Goodness that should be yours disdains the planned
Obeisances that only do it damage.
Take this less humble, yet more modest homage
Due you grace my waiting when I stand
Upon the threshold of your dear attention,
Holding no permit but an ancient pain
Almost worn thin like a repeated story
Retaining color past the comprehension
Of its narrator, me, who must remain
An interloper in love's territory.

Mardi Gras Morning

It was the wine speaking, but the wine spoke love,
at least, my love, not Jesus,
who would hold you close
like wind,
like water,
like sunlight.
It was my love, not Jesus, assuring
the power no human hands hold
playing "Keep Away" with our death
mutual, multi-faceted diamond
terrible gift of our God to mother His children
here in our hands letting us garrison each other's
breathing moist in our mouths
our two tongues talking and touching
where no one has touched us before, at least me,
soft at the lips or hard by the heart, or here
nearer and nearer the gardens humid
and hidden and to the tamper of taste
suffered only by those who suffer like Jesus,
ignorant knowing nobody speaks except Love.

Fiat

Eden is closed forever, if it was
Opened to us anytime anywhere,
And we who try to find it have more cause
For grief, I think, than Adam, forced to wear
The skins of guileless animals outside the gates
And watch Eve sweating, no longer clothed only
In delicate nakedness, lust and hates
Stuffing them both full, however finely.
At least they knew their state and did not try
To get back in. They saw the burning angel
And did not bait his flame. They had to die
And so walked toward their deaths austere and
Single. Yet from those gates we come back emptyhanded
Over and over foolish still, and branded.

Disgusted

No, I'm not here. My dog wags at a ghost.
I haunt the house I have since I was born.
No one can find me where I'm not even lost.
I'm here and yet I'm not. Why can't you learn.
We greet each other. You don't so much as see me.
You shake my hand. It's the wrong hand you shake.
You only think you think it's not. Waylay me?
Ha-ha, I'm somewhere else too. Go give the ache
To someone else too. 'Bye. I said Hello?
Excuse your ignorance and kiss my shadow,
If not my ass. Then please to come and go,
Ladies and gentlemen. It wouldn't aid you—
Not my address. See what you want to see.
Till otherwise, please sit in a damn tree!

Abstinence

The long weeks drag, lag, sag as if on crutches,
I count them on my fingers one by one.
Lent's a serious game we make up, no fun
At all, it turns out, though it gives us touches,
Smidges of holiness. Yet, given as much as
An inch, I'd hightail it ten miles, and run
Away from this season of soft sun
And luscious green when, contrary to the churches,
God doesn't seem to know it's Lent, by God!
Or, rather, it is Lent, spring, the year's heyday,
Not winter. Look out the window—every flower
Keeps faith, not me washed in the blood,
Till, heavy with abstinence, in crawls Good Friday
When Christ's pain, quicker than my own, wears slower.

Invocation

Hurricane, hurricane,
blow me away,
frail as a moth,
light as a leaf;
shake me loose from my skin,
blast me out of my bones,
dancing upon my humanness
grinding it into powder
less than the dust.
Sever me from my heart,
sunder me from my soul
till I am purer than angels,
sinless as God.

Aubade

FOR SOME FRIENDS AND A <u>FEW</u> RELATIONS

In the black belly of the bird
cawing to country bumpkins,
"This day is born
in the city of fools
one more poor son of a bitch
born to get himself done in!"

Had we soared in the bird's black belly
swooping down over some hick
cracking his prayer bones and crying,
"Save from what I know goddamn well will soon happen!"

Had we soared on the wings of the black bird
squawking over some dusty graveyard
where mourners mourn the flesh
stiff in the dirt as a rod
that will rise no more
Jesus! you would have had a communion of coffee and
      cinnamon.

Dark Cycle

No prayer or penitence, no positive thinking,
No science, reason, neither spells of magic,
No courtroom pleadings clever, deftly tragic,
No devil-may-care tricks like boisterous drinking,
No methods professorial and pedagogic
Can stave it off a breath, elude by blinking

Away the black dog as Churchill used to call
His intimate darkness, Lincoln knew it too,
Did Shakespeare? Did Jesus? As ounce by ounce
The verse and praises throbbed? And maybe Paul
Besought God thrice against it—yet finally knew
God stopped the sun one time, but only once.

Bach

IN MEMORIAM: THE OLD ORGAN

Roll up all music underneath the sky,
Then toss the manuscript out for a rock,
Like the monkeys pecking typewriters—by
Some miracle of chance, it will be Bach,
Whose name lacks rhyme in English or in music.
I look in vain for one only to cast
Aside each melody upon the basic
Rapture of counterpoint, which weaves and braids
The airs into a golden net to draw
Into itself tonalities, all shades,
Transporting us staid listeners into awe
With Sunday worship spiraled and crisscrossed
By Bach's bright signatures of Pentecost.

Meditation after an Interview

I speak myself, and my name
is only smoke
and less than smoke.

I say who I am, and my name
slips from my mouth
to become a word in a foreign tongue.

I explain myself, and my name,
turned witness against me,
puts questions I cannot answer.

I say myself, and my name
drifts out, a bright colored bubble
to splinter against the wind.

But if You say me, my Lord, my name
I meet in Your darkness and hear it
singing content in Your silence.

Bitter Song

Everything dies—animal, planet, star—
Death's seed implanted with life's direful semen,
Dark gospel translated to beast and human
(Given the difference!) I have heard no bar
Of joy in the dust of things as they are,
Such as is mimicked by sweet-throated women
And men gold-vested, but only the omen
As written on wind and fire and air.

So, I sit here in the small humid corner
Thin as the thread through a slim needle's eyelet,
Reading my navel in my belly's small girth
For want of another and better page-turner,
Hunching, grunting, and naked on the toilet,
Feeling my vast and my puny unworth.

Every Damn Time

If I left home to see my lover
I do not have,
my eyes would still turn back
to my lonesome bed.

If I took off
to visit my best friend
to cure me of solitude,
I would lament my dogs
who never say anything.

For I resemble my father
who longed to get away,
and started cursing as a gyp-joint
the first town he came to.

Yet now I am back home
the familiar pinches my feet,
I don't know where the hell I am,
and I want a drink.

Rivers

How innocent we all were,
speaking of death and murder,
cold over the river,
wishing for love to order
over the soft Susquehanna.

Beloved, my brother, where are you,
you curly-haired wonder I saw
running home crying to me
wild as the wide Missouri?

We shall all die too soon,
burning our breathing must wane,
winding clean down with the sun
searing the broad Ohio.

Burning, so brilliant the deeps,
footfalls descending the steps,
longing still sealing the lips,
nearer the banks of the Brazos,

Rio de Brazos de Dios,
river of rest and rescues,
bear me with lullabies,
safe to the arms of Jesus.

For Helen on Her Birthday

I do not kneel to you
(and yet, my dear, I do)
for who knows what God desires,
what reverence requires?
The heart of Eucharist
means no one except Christ.
And still I can pay homage
to none save God's one Image
to see Whom must be Heaven
itself, yet here the leaven
of human care are those
in whom we find repose,
at least a little while,
wherefore your glance, your smile
must serve the narrow space
I pass through till His face
may bless, have in His stead
Your hand light on my head.

Rubenstein's Melody in F

FOR J. M. L. M.

Beauty you loved—not beauty too proud,
Say, rather, loveliness, say charming things,
Boutiques and bracelets, miniatures, rings,
Babies in cribs and puppies in a mound
Of drowsiness or ladies groomed and gowned,
Crosses for pendants, and Strauss's honeyed strings.
Not at your funeral my sorrow spread its wings,
But in a shop with pretty wares around,

For beauty itself lives much too near the edge,
Province of death and terror, to allow
Your rest, and beauty bared to bone's the keep
Of worms and worship you could never hedge
With roses, daisies, Queen Anne's Lace when now
Your grave, dear heart, lies deep and deep and deep.

Sick

The body stops, starts, stops, starts once again,
This time for good, it looks like. I'll agree
It isn't very good at best, can't be.
No refund on this throw-away beer can.
But *carpe diem*, that stuff—better than
Nothing, far better than, in fact, to me.
And so, I hold my cookies, count to three,
And take my doctor's lousy medicine.

Lousier because sweet. I'm not that sick,
Just feel that way, partial to the attentions
I miss most times. Courteous shibboleth
Of those who greet the poorly, then turn quick
To wholesome ways, minding their little engines
That could, that could (how smoothly) puff toward death.

Death Song

Hear culex mosquitos sing in my ear,
Minute Bachs composing Komm Süsser Tod
Ad Major Gloria Dei, to God's great glory, where
No composer will find them later, save odd
Folk who may come to my puny grave
Where my bones will lie buried, providing
Nutrients to the living. Till then now
I lie near where my two dogs lie buried
Guarded by a stone St. Francis, who preached
To the wild creatures, God's Little Poor Man,
God's poor retard more likely, who reached
A credulous Pope's attention, as can
People of that ilk. Now those bones are less
Than dust, no longer feeding even the grass.

Tremulous

The slow fire burns, burned under the cold earth
All winter long when we could not tell
What lay under the snow wraps from the north.
Yet under silence silences will swell
Until they burst in thunder, platitude,
A lioness in the sun with eyes aglaze
Till fanned to metaphor, language renewed
By pain and terror clawing through cliches.
And when the fire blazes, the animal pounces,
The word beats into flesh, the old grows young—
Life goes confused: it leaps? it winces?
As Mary seeing finally her dead Lord strong
Was not sure how she felt, that spring bloomed greener than
    spring.
Her hurt love healed? Her longing keener?

A Mourning

I could be eased easier than the apple Eve
took from the tree untugged only touched and the
tender places open up offering all to a whisper
of flesh to a murmur of skin against skin to
delicacies dancing together.

You could be held for the holding lighter than leaves
touching like fingertips taking the pick of you
yielding wherever one would wandering over these
smooth joys of eyelid, tissue surrounding mouth
hollow of breast down slipping down toward tongue's
softest bruising.

We could be pilfered picked each in clean sight of the
other, one naked as bellies kissing needing no bridge
of a breath every space between them this night
narrowed to nothing, how much leaner than hounds how
much hungrier for the bones of thin human love.

Yet now we sleep safe from the nag and nudge of desire
smug as two corpses laid out drained of their sundry
fluids their pallidness painted and prettied up by the
smirking proprieties rubbing their hands trained in how
to impress those bereaved.

Villanelle for Buffy

Although she's eating well and wags her tail,
Sleeps well at night, barks loudly every morning,
My old dog's dying, dying like us all.

The seed of death's in her and was and will
Be born in everything that stirs as warning,
Although she's eating well and wags her tail.

It's not her like, poor thing, that will prevail.
(She's happy, I suppose, no fear aborning.)
My old dog's dying, dying like us all

Who mourn ourselves as much as her—she'd wail
Mostly for food despite my loved returning.
Although she's eating well and wags her tail,

No one—and she is certainly too small—
Can laugh down death who laughs down mortal scorning.
My old dog's dying, dying like us all

Who run at last into that iron wall
Whose gate is locked until that bright Day's burning.
Although she's eating well and wags her tail,
My old dog's dying, dying like us all.

Elegy Long Time in the Making

FOR BESSIE MONROE EBAUGH

We sit together. Forty years ago
We sat the same way, we such good girls prim
As you were proper, keeping minds in trim.
Those days we studied English under you
Until time took us further than we knew.
Today we sit, sit in a course more grim,
Scarcely however for credit or for whim,
One you've not taught before, but teach it now.
Now some robed man who, saying much, says little
About your iron mercies, kind as you are, lady
Of duty lived—and died. Bach's only breaths
Himself, it seems, these moments breaking brittle
Against you, stumbled, you of step most steady,
May your mere dying grade us on our deaths.

Elegy for a Good Ole Boy

Poor ole Billy Carter,
who should've been smarter
'n done what he oughter,
he made my heart melt
'cause I knowed what he felt—
"I done things I shouldn't
'n I caught the blame,
done things I should (Wouldn't
you know?), caught the same."
They taken his beers.
Lord God, a few years
sprinted pasted 'n he died,
saving big brother's hide,
not his own. Still, 'n all, well,
guess he don't roast in Hell.
So, each man take off your tie.
In the Sweet Bye 'n Bye.
Lord, give him the cheer
of many a beer.
There it won't hurt his liver
'n nobody don't ever
have no hangover.

Elegy for Nina

We left you lying in a lean land,
your death laconic as the clods that spilled
around the edges of your fake grass blanket
on which the coffin waited
blatant as a creditor

demanding from the poverty of your life
whitted from your riches
wary of overstatement.
Turning alike from flesh and spirit,
sex and God hyperboles
in your stiff prose,

wearing the livery of yourself,
you strode through life,
doing your kindnesses by counting on your fingers,
stuttering over the ABC's of love,
unlettered in its nuances—

I think you have stalked into the heaven
you could not imagine
with all your graces
worn wrong side out.

Elegy for Judith Resnick

O, let her lie there. Do not bring her up,
Up from her bedding on the ocean floor.
Give her body no trouble any more
Than it has known already. Water's crop
Today, she was the fire's. You should not reap
Yet one more time what won't belong to air.
That is too much, too much of you to dare.
So, that which water claims, let water keep.

Although it had no claim in the first place
On her, nor had she any business, surely,
With any elements but melodies
She used to play, and none at all in space.
Forgive me. I presume. Yet she's paid dearly.
So, leave the waves her lovely bones for keys.

Meditation on Mortality

Old dog panting laps summer afternoon
away, dripping like honey to the grass
as long sighs of cicadas soon and soon
inhale, exhale to silences that kiss
old listener away in a soft dream
never fulfilled, yet so never released,
held in a timelessness no facts consume
to dull reality of being pinned and placed.
Old dog shall die and so old listener shall,
two motes adrift upon the seasonal sea
greening and praising over and over till
God calls earth to a halt when mortal eye
darkening always, brightens forever.
Old dog relaxes, belches, hearty sleeper.
Old listener gets up for beer and supper.

Meditation at a Funeral

The air is peaceful. We don't see the coffin.
Well, I suppose the body's been cremated.
The organ starts, and we are serenaded
By "For All the Saints," a hymn I've often
Heard sung before. It touches me. I soften,
Reminded of my mother's service. Aided
By cane, a fat, old woman's just paraded
Down the aisle as if she owned it (toughen
Up, Heart!) reminding me of her. It's scary
The way things fall sometimes. I wonder if
She loved me. The red-haired acolyte is younger
Than my red-headed nephew who helped carry
Her casket. I go out—not faith, but life,
Delaying action against death, grown stronger.

If I Had Wheels or Love

CHIEFLY FOR JOANNE AVINGER

I could make prayers or poems on and on,
Relax or labor all the summer day,
If I had wheels or love, I would be gone.

Spinning along the roadsides into dawn,
Feeling the flesh of lovers whom I'd lay
I could make prayers or poems on and on.

Whistling the hours by me as they drone,
Kissed on my breast and belly where I'd play
If I had wheels or love, I would be gone.

Over the next horizon toward the sun,
Deep in the shadows where I found the way
I could make prayers or poems on and on.

Along the country backroads flower-strewn,
Fondling your flanks, my dear, made clouds from clay.
If I had wheels or love, I would be gone.

Cool as the evening is and soft as fawn,
Warm as my fiddling fingers when they say
I could make prayers or poems on and on.
If I had wheels or love, I would be gone.

Index of First Lines

345

Index of Titles

Maud Lipscomb

About the Author

VASSAR MILLER was born in Houston, Texas, in 1924 and has lived in that city all her life. Handicapped by cerebral palsy since birth, she has overcome its disabilities with energy and courage. She began writing as a child, encouraged by her father, who brought home from his office the typewriter upon which she wrote her first poems, and by her stepmother, who taught her to read and write and enabled her to attend public schools. Miller earned B.S. and M.A. degrees from the University of Houston and taught creative writing at a private academy in Houston. She has traveled extensively and, besides her own books of poetry, has published *Despite This Flesh*, an anthology of poetry and stories about the disabled. Her poetry was nominated for the Pulitzer Prize in 1961, and her work has appeared in more than fifty anthologies and hundreds of periodicals, both in English and in translation.